Where Wind meets Wave

Also by Caroline Fyffe

Prairie Hearts Series
Where The Wind Blows
Before The Larkspur Blooms
West Winds of Wyoming
Under a Falling Star
Whispers on the Wind
Where Wind Meets Wave

McCutcheon Family Series
Montana Dawn
Texas Twilight
Mail-Order Brides of the West: Evie
Mail-Order Brides of the West: Heather
Moon Over Montana
Mail-Order Brides of the West: Kathryn
Montana Snowfall
Texas Lonesome

Stand Alone Western Historical
Sourdough Creek

Stand Alone Contemporary Women's Fiction
Three And A Half Minutes

Where Wind meets Wave

A Prairie Hearts Novel
Book Six

Caroline Fyffe

Where Wind Meets Wave
Copyright © 2016 by Caroline Fyffe
All rights reserved by the author.

www.carolinefyffe.com

Where Wind Meets Wave is a work of fiction. Names, characters, places, and incidents are either products of the author's imagination or used fictitiously. Any resemblance to actual events, locals, or persons, living or dead, is wholly coincidental.

No part of this publication can be reproduced or transmitted in any form or by any means, electronic or mechanical, recording, by information storage and retrieval or photocopied, without permission in writing from Caroline Fyffe.

Edited by Bulletproof Editing & Lustre Editing
Cover design by Kelli Ann Morgan
Interior book design by Bob Houston eBook Formatting

Proudly Published in the United States of America

ISBN # 978-1-944617-01-1

About the Book

Drawn from Wyoming Territory for the first time in his life, Jake Costner sets off to find his destiny, leaving his love behind in Logan Meadows. *Where Wind Meets Wave*, Book 6 of the Prairie Hearts series by *USA Today* bestselling author Caroline Fyffe, will keep you on the edge of your seat.

Discovering his saloon-girl mother has known all along who sired him, Jake takes his fate into his own hands and travels away from the only family he's ever known. Unaware of what awaits him at the end of his train ride, Jake discovers not only a dying father, but a surprise that will change his life—forever. More is on the line than returning to Logan Meadows, where Daisy Smith awaits the wedding he's promised.

Given new awakenings, bitter sorrow, and a daring escape, will Jake return a whole man? Or will the happiness he and Daisy have been building for the last two years be lost where wind meets wave?

Dedication

*For my wonderful son, Matthew, for all the help and support.
You keep me on track.
Love you!*

Chapter One

October 1883, Somewhere between Wyoming and Oregon, Union Pacific Rail Line

The clickety-clack of the train wheels agitated Jake's ragged nerves and kept him from falling asleep. Eyes gritty with fatigue ached as if a ten-pound weight were laid atop each lid. Bracing his boot on the back of the seat in front of him, he tried to get comfortable. His five-day trip was about to come to an end. Rest on a solid surface would be welcome.

What will my life look like this time tomorrow?

The door between the two passenger cars opened and a porter carrying a lantern stepped inside, the amber glow infusing the dark space. He was older, heavyset, his uniform rumpled and worn. He ambled down the aisle, glancing at the sleeping passengers.

When he got to Jake, he stopped. "You haven't gotten much sleep since you boarded, young man."

Jake shrugged. The man was right, but what could he say?

The porter chuckled. "Didn't mean no offense. Just gets mighty lonely on the night shift. All the passengers snoring away and me havin' ta stay awake. I noticed you haven't been one of 'em."

"I reckon you're right," Jake whispered. He wished he could be one of the sleepers.

"Some people don't cotton to the rocking motion. Never get used to it."

That was only part of the problem. "Thanks, but I'll be getting off tomorrow. I appreciate your concern."

The man smiled and moved on, leaving Jake to his pondering.

Tomorrow was just around the corner. What would he find? Would his father even be able to talk? Had his sickness gotten worse? Or had he died?

At the thought, a flash of molten fire ignited in his belly, but he tamped it back.

After all these years, he'd meet his father. Jake's mother had sworn she hadn't known who his father was. Being a saloon girl for most of her adult life, she'd entertained more than her fair share of men. That falsehood had been just another in her long list of lies.

Jake pushed back the anger gnawing at his gut. Now, as if in a dream, he was about to meet the man whose blood flowed through his own veins.

Provided he arrived in time.

The train jerked violently and then rocked back and forth before chugging onward. This section of track through the Willamette Valley to the Oregon coast seemed rougher and the train had slowed, sometimes almost to a crawl.

Several seats in front of him, a burly man who'd been snoring for the past hour sat up at the disturbance and looked around. He cast one questioning look at Jake before settling back onto his seat. Farther up the car, a mother, huddled with three children in a pile of arms and legs, whispered and shushed them back to sleep.

Jake swallowed and turned his gaze to the deep, foreboding darkness on the other side of the window. He'd never been out of Wyoming Territory.

Jake Costner.

He couldn't get used to thinking of himself in those terms. For his whole life, he'd been Jake. Just Jake.

What's Daisy doing now? The question was never far from his mind. He glanced down at the book resting on the seat beside him. *The Last of the Mohicans.* Daisy's parting gift, but he was far too preoccupied to read.

On the eve before he'd departed Wyoming, he'd lain awake for hours, keyed up and uncomfortable. Chase and Jessie had insisted he and his best friend, Gabe, spend the night in the large, rustic ranch house with them, even though the two young men normally lived in the bunkhouse with the other ranch hands. Jake hadn't wanted to put out his adoptive family, hadn't wanted to make a bigger deal of his leaving in search of his father than it already was. But Jessie usually had her way when the subject in question was her family and making them feel special.

She'd gone to great lengths preparing his going-away supper, cooking up all his favorites. Pot roast, mashed potatoes and gravy, pumpkin pie with thick, sweet cream on top. Using the buggy, he'd picked up Daisy in Logan Meadows and brought her out to the ranch.

A hefty sigh escaped. That evening felt like ten years ago instead of four days. Then later that night, when he'd taken Daisy back into town, he'd driven off the road where they could say their good-byes in private. They'd kissed under the moonlight, the farewell bittersweet.

She hadn't said as much, but he knew she hadn't wanted him to go. She was frightened, worried he'd find something better and not return. Didn't she know how much he loved her? Would give his life for her? Just as soon as he had this business behind him and returned, he'd erase all the doubt from her mind.

He dragged his thoughts away from Daisy.

The train would reach the coast first thing in the morning. Would his father still be alive? He wished the letter his mother had brought to town had gone into a little more detail. As exciting as the prospect was, Jake didn't like walking in blind. If he and Daisy were lucky enough to have a son or daughter, he'd be a good father, watch over any child of his carefully.

Jake withdrew the post from his pocket and took the missive from the envelope. He searched for something he might have missed. After all these years of wondering who the man was, the prospect of actually meeting him now had Jake's mouth as dry as sand—or perhaps the hours he'd been riding this iron horse were responsible.

"Newport! Yaquina Bay!" a deep baritone voice called out.

Jake jerked awake as the train slowly rolled to a stop.

The small family several seats in front of him squirmed in excitement, their faces and hands pressed to the grimy glass.

He glanced outside. The cloud-covered sun was midway past the gray horizon. He'd finally fallen asleep, only to wake much later than normal.

"I believe this is your stop, young fella."

The same porter from last night stood at his seat. His smile revealed a missing front tooth Jake hadn't noticed before.

"Pick up your travel chest at—"

"Don't have a trunk," Jake said, interrupting him. "Just this bag, my saddlebags, and a horse."

"In that case, when you go to retrieve your horse, be aware a prison camp sits close to where you'll be collecting your animal. Best not hang around. A few months back, a civilian was almost killed when he got curious, crossed the tracks, and approached the fence."

That was a term Jake wasn't familiar with. "Prison camp? Here on the coast?"

"Yes, sir. Hard-core criminals being transported up from San Francisco by ship to meet another vessel bound for Alaska. They'll live out their sentences in a gold mine on the Kenai Peninsula."

"You mean lives, don't you?"

The conductor nodded and then turned to go. "Pretty much. The stories the guards bring back freeze your blood." Ambling away, the man stopped to chat with the family now hopping up and down with excitement like a bunch of prairie dogs.

Jake stood, stretched, and worked out the kinks in his neck and back. He hadn't eaten much on the way, and now a ferocious hunger burned in his belly. Once he picked up his horse, he'd find some food and a bathhouse. Get cleaned up.

After reaching overhead, he lifted down his soft leather saddlebag and tossed it over one shoulder, then went for his bag. Covering the distance in eight paces, he arrived at the front and took the three narrow steps, descending into the chilly morning air, unaware of what his future might hold.

He paused and looked around. Coastal mountains to the north and south were small compared to what he was used to in Wyoming. A gloomy slate-gray sky, so different from the vivid, welcoming blue of home, hung low over the land and then disappeared into the Pacific Ocean. The salty air had a biting chill and smelled like rotting fish. Gusts of wind moved women's skirts and bonnets as they rushed into the arms of their waiting family and friends.

Everything about this place seemed to want to drive him away—the wind pushing him back toward the train, the clouds pressing down upon his body, the mocking cry of the seagulls.

Go home, they all said. *You don't belong here.*

Feeling alone, Jake pulled down his hat and started for the rear of the train, the weight of his .45 Colt, the only familiar sense keeping him grounded.

Had he arrived in time? Or had he made this long trip for nothing?

Chapter Two

Jake waited with several men at the stock car as a railroad employee began unloading the horses. One by one, they came down the slanted ramp. A flighty blood bay was led down first and handed over to a large fellow. Next came two stocky quarter horses, by the looks of their conformation.

As Jake waited, he glanced across another set of tracks to an old train car surrounded by a tall barbed-wire fence, the strands only an inch apart. The two men who stood guard looked more disreputable than the two inside. Their tattered US army uniforms had seen better days. The prisoners wore loose-fitting black-striped pants and shirts, as well as small striped hats.

"Your horse?"

Jerked out of his gawking, Jake spun around. "Yeah, how did you know?"

"You're the last bloke here. One horse, one man."

Jake took Joker's lead rope.

"Wait one minute and I'll get his gear." The man hurried off.

Jake turned his attention back to the two convicts who sat listlessly on a long bench. Nothing else occupied the compound except a fire pit and a rickety outhouse. The men stared off at the far horizon, which had a glimpse of Yaquina Bay.

The dark hair and large shoulders of the fellow on the end caught Jake's attention. He didn't have a clear look at the man's face, but something about the sharpness of his profile made Jake stare.

The man swayed and then mumbled to the skinny fellow beside him.

Jake sucked in a breath of surprise. *Dalton Babcock?* Could that possibly be? Or was the man a look-alike?

Indecision warred inside Jake. Why would Dalton be a prisoner? He'd arrived in Logan Meadows last April, the day the Pacific Union train wrecked at Three Pines Turn, one of three men hired by the First National Bank of Denver to transport a large amount of money to San Francisco.

In the beginning of this month, Albert Preston, the sheriff of Logan Meadows, had received a letter from Dalton. He was doing well but planned to come back to Logan Meadows as soon as he finished his current job assignment. Make the town his home.

What had happened? Had he committed a crime and been tried and sentenced that quickly? That outcome didn't seem possible. He was a good man with a good reputation.

"This is it," the stockman said, setting Jake's saddle, blanket, and bridle next to him on the ground.

Troubled, all Jake could do was nod. Finally, after checking his gear, he found his voice. "I hear those prisoners are bound for Alaska."

"That's right. Just as soon as the merchant ship returns."

"When would that be?"

"Don't know. Maybe tomorrow, maybe next month. Just depends on the weather the ship encounters on its return voyage." The man shielded his eyes from the sun that had peeked out from a cloud, looking at the camp. "Unlucky chaps. It's no secret the conditions are mighty ugly where they're going—and that's before the bitter cold sets in. I guess it's a fitting punishment for hardened killers." The man eyed him suspiciously. "Why do you want to know?"

"Just curious." Jake bent over for his saddle blanket and tossed it up on Joker's back.

"You best not be curious anymore. Those guards strike faster than a rattlesnake. Stay out of their way."

Jake stared him in the eye. "I'm not interested in criminals."

Dalton Babcock, if that's him, is no criminal. That's the only surety of the situation.

Jake took one more quick look in time to see the man slump to the side. He'd have fallen from the bench if the small man next to him hadn't grasped his shirtsleeve and pulled him upright.

Was he sick? Hurt?

Maybe the fellow wasn't Dalton after all. The man Jake knew was strong and tall. Fierce, with those piercing eyes the color of caramel or gold, like an eagle's. He was a strong-willed man too. One who believed in law and order, or so he'd thought.

Would Dalton have turned to crime in the short time since he wrote the letter to Albert? Or had someone done this to him? This man was sick, or hurt. If that was Dalton, then Jake was certain something was wrong.

A need for answers pushed up in Jake's chest. Somehow, some way, he needed to find out what was going on—before the ship arrived.

Chapter Three

"**P**ay attention, Freddy!"

Adaline Costner gripped the ruler she used to illustrate her point when she'd much rather wield the tool to rap the unruly eight-year-old on his knuckles. With revulsion, she snatched away the spitball he was about to flick at Jasper, the family's house cat asleep on a parlor chair, and dropped the soggy ball of paper into the trash can before she discreetly wiped her fingers on her skirt.

"You failed your last mathematics test. No wonder your parents are none too happy with your studies. You need to take your assignments seriously."

I can't afford to lose this job. Once Papa is gone, Courtney will depend on me to keep us out of the poorhouse.

Her heart trembled with love for her dying father at the same time her frustration with him lingered. *Why hadn't he been more truthful about our finances? I'm no longer a child to be protected.*

What her father didn't know was that for the past year, Mr. Hexum, Newport's local banker, had been pressuring her to marry him. If she did, the fox-eyed financier promised to forgive all of her father's loans. Hexum, in his late thirties, had taken over the bank when his own father had passed away a few years ago. Since then, more properties had been foreclosed on than in the bank's entire history. For that reason alone, Adaline wouldn't marry him.

Still, his sneaky expressions and the way he looked at her made her skin crawl. Thank goodness her father owned their house. Money from selling the only home she'd known would keep her and Courtney sustained for a good long time. Give her a chance to figure out what they should do.

She pointed to the pencil marks. "Freddy, I've explained this problem three times, and I can tell you haven't listened to a word I've said. This is Monday, and your test is on Wednesday. You'd best listen up."

"Sorry, Miss Costner. I got distracted."

Freddy's remorseful expression didn't fool her one bit. She sighed and gazed around the beautifully decorated room. The Bennetts were one of the richest and most influential families in Newport.

"We'll begin again," she said, laying the ruler on the paper. "We know Jasper's tail is six inches long." She put a pencil mark on the paper at the end of the ruler, and then at the six-inch mark. "We also know a seagull's tail is about two inches long." She marked the corresponding spot. "How much longer is Jasper's tail than a seagull's?"

Freddy studied the ruler atop the paper.

She thought this time he would make the connection and count the extra inches right there in front of his face. After a moment, she ticked off the extra four inches with her finger.

"Freddy? Do you know?"

"Nope."

"You must! We covered much more difficult problems last week." She counted the inches for him. "Four! The cat's tail is four inches longer."

There was no way Freddy would pass his exam. The thing was, he couldn't care less. Her teaching strengths were English and writing, but with the approaching test, she was spending their entire daily hour on math.

When the parlor clock chimed, Adaline ignored the dread smoldering in her stomach and gathered her books. "For tomorrow, I'd like you to go over this several times, and then make up three new word problems using the ruler. Write them out for me to check. Be sure you know the answers. I'll be here at five after three, so don't be late."

Mrs. Bennett's steps echoed from the stairway as she ascended from the store below. "All finished?" she asked, coming into the room. She smiled lovingly at Freddy and then turned a stern eye on Adaline.

Being the only child of the well-to-do mercantile owners, Freddy was spoiled rotten. He was late to arrive every day. Stole candy from the store below and ate until he was blue in the face. Adaline had even caught him in more than a few lies. As had his mother . . . but Mrs. Bennett never seemed to mind, saying boys would be boys. Only when he brought home failing papers did she take a severe tone with Freddy, but more often she questioned Adaline's teaching methods and tutoring qualifications.

"Yes, we are," Adaline responded, her books in her arm and her bag slung over her shoulder. She needed to get home. Being away too long worried her.

"How's Freddy doing?"

The same question she asks every day. "I believe we're making progress. I do wish he would try a little harder, though.

He's capable when he sets his mind to something." From the corner of her eye, she saw the boy smirk.

"That's good to hear." Mrs. Bennett came forward, money in hand. "Math is so important for every aspect in our daily living. Don't you agree, Adaline?"

Today was payday. Adaline held out her hand as the woman reached forward. The two dollars a month added up. Being questioned like this almost felt as if she were being scolded.

She nodded. "Yes, I do. And especially for shopkeepers." As she moved toward the upstairs door, she said, "I'll see you tomorrow, Freddy."

Turning, she saw Freddy poke at Jasper with the sharp end of his pencil. The sleepy cat sprang to his feet and darted away.

Adaline knew exactly how the poor animal felt.

After cleaning himself up and buying a meal, Jake reined up in front of a two-story house, covered from top to bottom in shingles, a style of construction he'd never before seen. The homes were narrow and closer together than he was used to seeing in Wyoming.

If he'd known his father lived in town, and so little riding would be involved, he wouldn't have gone to the trouble and expense of bringing Joker. As it was, he was glad for the moral support, even if only from his horse.

Dismounting, he flicked his reins over the knee-high rail fence. A handful of chickens pecked in the dirt at the base of the porch of the run-down house.

As a young boy, Jake had imagined his father as a profitable rancher with herds several thousand strong, a sheriff keeping the peace, or a banker with tills filled with money. As Jake grew older, his perception changed; more realistically, his pa could be a gambler, or maybe even an outlaw. Someone taking up with the likes of his ma would surely be closer to that.

Over the last year, Jake realized he didn't care what his father's occupation was, what mattered changed to what kind of a man he was. Honest and trustworthy, or a slouch and a cheat? Wouldn't be long before he found out.

Taking a deep breath, he strode up the walk, the fried oysters he'd tried at the restaurant an hour before turning heavy in his stomach. They might be a delicacy around here, but he'd take a good Wyoming-bred steak any day of the week. With hat in hand, he lifted a fist and knocked.

A few moments passed before the door opened to display a middle-aged woman. Her hair was pulled back in a bun. Her apron needed washing.

"You're the boy?" she asked.

He nodded and removed his hat. "Yes, ma'am."

"Good. You've come in time," she said with neither a smile nor a frown. "I'll go see if he's awake." She led Jake into the parlor where filled bookcases lined every open wall. "Wait here."

Not knowing where to put his hat, Jake kept it in his hands. His nose picked up a warm, cloying scent associated with sickness that made his stomach clench even more so than from the oysters.

The woman ascended the stairs on the far side of the parlor, her labored steps clomping loudly. A long, rattling cough sounded from upstairs.

Jake glanced around the room but stayed in the spot she'd left him. The house was quiet except for the cough he'd just heard.

"Mr. Costner is awake and wants to see you," the woman called down the stairway. "You may come up." She waited at the top of the landing where more bookshelves filled the area.

Jake had never seen so many books in one place, not even in Miss Canterbury's bookshop back in Logan Meadows.

"This way."

He followed down a short hallway to an open door.

A man was propped up on several pillows in a bed on the far side of the room, clutching a red-spotted handkerchief in one hand. His face, although pasty and sunken now, had at one time been handsome. His eyes were alert and keen.

My father!

The woman gestured to a chair next to the bed. "Will you need anything else, Mr. Costner?" she asked.

Costner looked at him. "Would you like anything to eat or drink?"

Hearing his father's voice for the first time rocked Jake. It was deep and soft spoken. Jake shook his head.

"That will be all, Mrs. Torry. Thank you."

Jake watched the woman leave before crossing the room and lowering himself into the bedside chair. After all the years of wondering about his father, he couldn't think of how to begin, couldn't make his mouth open an inch.

James Costner let loose a barrage of coughing into his handkerchief, coughing that felt like it rattled the walls. "Hello, Jake," he finally said. "Thank you for making the trip. I've wondered about you for years."

Jake looked away, his jaw clenched tightly. *He's wondered about me for years? When he knew where to find me? Must not have wondered too hard.*

"I know what you're thinking."

"No, you don't." His first words to his father were opposition. How fitting. "Consumption?"

Costner leaned back into his pillows, spent. "No. That's what the doctors thought at first. I'm glad it's not, because that disease is very contagious. I have lung cancer." He cleared his throat, then took up a different cloth sitting on the bedspread and wiped his sweaty forehead. "From what I hear, it's not an easy way to die."

"Surgery?"

"Too late for that."

Was Jake supposed to feel sorry for him? If that was the expectation, he was having a hard time of it.

"You look good. A strapping young man. Like I used to be. By God, I'm glad to finally meet you."

Did you love her? Or was I just a product of a roll in the hay? "Wish I could say the same."

"But you can't?"

It didn't matter that Jake would like to rail at the man, tell him what a disgusting human being he was for leaving a woman in the family way. His ma had been just as young as he was now, if not younger, when she'd conceived.

"Why did you want to meet me now—before you died? By my way of thinking, you could've sent for me anytime in the past twenty-one years. But you didn't."

Costner shrugged. "I'm not proud of what happened all those years ago."

They stared at each other but Jake remained silent. He wouldn't ask anything from this man—especially not an apology. Would Costner even say he was sorry for what he'd done?

"I never meant to hurt her, or you. I got scared, wasn't ready to settle down. I had ambition." He lifted his hand and slowly reached in Jake's direction in a feeble gesture of supplication, but let it fall back to the bed. "Things to accomplish."

Maybe it was too late to fix their history. The man in bed was dying. No matter what he'd done or how wrong he'd been, the past was past. All that was left for them both was the present. And not much of that either.

"How long?" he gestured to the blood-stained handkerchief in his father's hand.

Costner gave a small cough into the cloth. "A matter of weeks—or could be only days. Don't know."

"Then I guess we best get talkin'. I only came for answers, nothin' else."

Costner's gaze shifted to the window but quickly came back to Jake's face. His chin edged up. "What would you like to know?"

Everything. What do you think it's like going through life without a name?

"Why not start with telling me who you are? Where your people are from." *My people too.*

A sadness passed over the man's face, but Jake wasn't moved in the least.

"Sunnyside, Michigan. I broke my mother's heart when I struck out west when I was twenty-three. I'd think many Costners still live there. My parents owned a partnership in a store with my uncle and aunt. They're good, God-fearing people."

Michigan? He'd hardly even heard of the place, let alone knew where the state was located in terms of the whole country.

I have blood relatives. A burning started in his heart and radiated out, a feeling of excitement mixed with dread. Like knowing Christmas was tomorrow, but also knowing nothing under the saloon tree would have your name.

"Last time I knew, they were still alive, but that was long ago."

"What are you?" Jake asked, feeling the sand beneath his feet firming considerably. "What did you do for a living?"

"Your grandparents believed in education. Made sure I had a good one. I'm certain you noticed my collection of books in the parlor and on the landing. When I was a kid, I'd read the day away when I wasn't stocking shelves in the store. Loved the written word so much, I wanted to be around writers. So I went into journalism. You know what that is?"

Damn him. Jake knew, but only because he'd overheard the long word over breakfast in the Silky Hen last week and asked Gabe the meaning. Journalism was writing articles and advertisements for the newspaper and such.

"Yeah, I know," he said low, hoping his father didn't ask for the definition.

Costner coughed and then reached for the glass of water on his bedside table. He took a short drink and then set it back.

"I started out typesetting for the local newspaper in Sunnyside. Long, long hours and tedious work. And a tongue-lashing if you made a tiny mistake. Still, desiring to become a journalist, I kept at it, even though I hated the job. I read other papers and saw a position open in a small town in Nebraska. Wrote a letter and packed my bags when I got a reply. That was the last I've seen of my people."

How could he just up and leave? He had a family. Didn't he know how precious that was? A mother, father, aunts, and uncles. Jake couldn't understand his father's thinking. He'd longed just to know who he was.

"I worked there for over three years. The owner hired and fired several men for the reporting position he'd promised to me in the letter. He kept saying I wasn't ready yet. He needed me to typeset but said that I'd be a writer, a reporter—someday. Well, you know what they say about someday . . ."

Unmoved, Jake stared. "It never comes."

Costner nodded. "That's correct. I became dejected. That's when I met your mama. She was young and sweet, made me feel important. I liked her attention. We got involved, and she began talking about marriage. Soon after, she said she was expecting. I panicked. I wasn't ready for a family. I had dreams. Things to accomplish. Ambitions that felt important to a young man. That night, I packed a bag and headed out, to who knew where. I was sick of working for pennies, breaking my back, and ruining my eyesight. I couldn't afford a wife and child on the pittance I made. So I headed west."

Jake clenched his fists. Hearing the story twice didn't make him understand any better. Empathy for his mother, Marlene, filled him. If Costner weren't already dying, then he would teach him a lesson he'd never forget.

"Why didn't you go back to Michigan?" he gritted out. "Back to your family?"

"And have my father say I told you so? He begged me not to leave. I couldn't show him that after all the time I'd been gone, I still hadn't achieved the career I wanted. I had to keep going, to keep trying. I didn't want him to laugh in my face."

And well he should have, the fool you were. "How did you know where to find me?" Jake couldn't let things rest until he knew everything.

Costner opened his mouth to reply but a racking cough doubled him over. Several moments passed before he could speak.

Grudgingly, Jake handed him his glass of water.

"I fled Nebraska because of what Marlene had told me; I left without my pay. Several months later, I stopped running and found a job washing dishes in a café. I wrote to my old boss, asking for the pay he owed me. Mostly, he was honest, and I knew he'd send what I had coming. I needed that money. Marlene must have asked him or seen the letter. That's the only way I can figure how she learned where I was. She wrote, begging me to reconsider. Said she'd run off, wanting to spare her parents the shame of their daughter having a child out of wedlock. But I was young and stupid, sleeping in boxcars or barns." He rubbed a hand over his face. "I'm not proud of what I did. How I let you both down. Once I'd set out, there was no going back."

Disgust curled Jake's lip.

"She tried a handful of times to reach me with her letters. After you were born, she wrote to tell me about my son. By then, I knew she was working saloons." He shook his head. "Her last note, years ago, said she was in a town called Valley Springs. She didn't want anything more than me contacting you. After that, I moved on. When I wrote just two months ago, I hoped you both were still there."

Drained, Jake closed his eyes. Stampeding emotions brought up all the times his mother, in a drunken rant, said he didn't have a pa. That she didn't know who he was.

No wonder. In her mind, that was the truth.

He couldn't recall a time before the saloons, the whiskey, the men. Perhaps they had enjoyed some good times, but he'd been too young to remember. At least he hadn't been conceived in a saloon. She'd been in love with James Costner, wanted them to be a family, and had fought for him. That, at least, was something.

Unable to remain in the same room with the man any longer, he stood and reached for his hat he'd set on the dresser when the sound of a door opening downstairs stilled his feet.

"Pa," a high-pitched female voice called. "I'm home."

Chapter Four

At the girlish voice coming from downstairs, Jake cut his gaze back to Costner, a burst of heat squeezing his chest. *Pa?*

Footsteps hurried up the stairs as Costner's gaze met his. "Yes, you have a sister. Actually two. You're about to meet the oldest."

Jake's hand curled into a fist. He couldn't call this man father. Chase had said not to rush things; understanding needs time to grow. After hearing the history, Jake didn't think he'd ever want it to.

"You couldn't accept the responsibility of a wife and child, and that's why you ran away only to do just that?"

Costner blinked at Jake's hard tone.

Jake stood when a tall young woman appeared in the doorway. She wore a prim white blouse and a blue skirt, the length of which showed the slim ankles of her black boots. Thick, dark blond hair hung down her back, the front pulled up in some sort of style. Several books rested in one arm, and she held a glass in the other hand. By the expression in her eyes, she knew exactly who he was.

"Don't be shy, Adaline, honey," Costner said after a loud round of coughing. He lowered the handkerchief. "Come meet Jake. He arrived a little while ago."

She assessed him a moment, then came forward slowly. Passing him without a word, she handed her father the glass.

"Drink some, Papa. It's fresh," she said, sliding a wary blue-eyed glance toward Jake. She pressed the back of her hand to her father's forehead and frowned. "You're warm. Drink the entire glass, please."

To oblige her, Costner downed the rest and gave her a tentative smile. "Adaline takes good care of me."

His words brought a smile to her lips. "Mrs. Torry does that. I just help."

His sister. He had a sister. Hard for him to believe. Of all the things he'd imagined about the father he never knew, having a sister or brother wasn't one of them.

"Jake, would you bring that other chair over here so Adaline can join us? I'd like to speak with you both."

Snapped out of his surprise, Jake crossed the room and took hold of another straight-back chair. Bringing the furniture over, he set it next to his.

Two sisters? The man could have given me a heads-up.

Warmth built in his chest when he wondered if they'd be a family, or once Jake went back to Logan Meadows, whether his sisters would want nothing to do with him.

"Thank you," Costner said. "Both of you get comfortable. Jake, this is Adaline, your half sister. She's exceptionally bright. Puts all the boys to shame." He gestured to the books Adaline had sat on the foot of his bed. "She's a tutor, and also works in the mercantile."

"Papa, *please*. He doesn't want to hear this trumped-up praise. And neither do I."

"It's not trumped up," Costner said, his lips pulling up at the corners, but his eyes held something else. Guilt. Regret. "You're very accomplished. As I'm sure your brother is."

Heat rushed to Jake's face. He dropped his gaze to his hands folded in his lap, annoyed at the prick of shame. *I can read now, thanks to Gabe. I have nothing to be embarrassed about. Easy to think, difficult to do.* He felt Adaline's gaze on the side of his face. He turned and met her eye to eye.

A tiny smile curved her lips. "I turned seventeen in September. How old are you?"

"Twenty-one." He was impressed. She had to know plenty about many subjects, not just reading and writing, in order to do what she did at such a young age. "You're a tutor?" he went on, feeling the need to fill the awkward silence.

"Surely you noticed all the books everywhere. What else could I be but a bookworm?" She glanced at the shelves in the hallway and laughed. "I love to read. My father calls me a tutor because he'd like to see me go into academia. I'm really a part-time store clerk at the mercantile, and I fill in when I can at the restaurant."

Jake gave her a small nod. Yes, he could see she was clever. Pretty too. He liked her face, her expressions, and the way her smile made him feel.

I have a sister! Two! I'm part of a family.

What other surprises would this trip bring him?

Adaline liked Jake. He was quiet and a bit shy, but the glimmer in his eye when their gazes connected gave her the feeling she wasn't in this situation alone. Perhaps the future would work itself out. He was tall, handsome, and she liked his strong jaw and observant eyes.

Her father straightened against his pillow. "What about you, Jake? Do you like to read?"

Feeling protective, Adaline protested, instinctively knowing this situation was hard on her new brother. "Of course he does, Papa. Everyone does."

Jake chuckled, although the sound didn't hold much mirth. "Truth is, I'd much rather be out riding herd."

Adaline nodded. "Nothing wrong with that."

"I *do* read," he said quickly. "I've read *The Tell-Tale Heart* by Edgar Allan Poe. And I brought along a copy of *The Last of the Mohicans.*"

She smiled approvingly. *Well done.* "*The Tell-Tale Heart* is one of my favorites, Jake. Scares me every time." Hearing him chuckle, she felt her face warm.

"Does me too. Where's the other, ah—sister? Does she still attend school?"

"She does. And her name is Courtney. This is her last year, though. After classes, she works for Mrs. Britton, a woman in her eighties who doesn't get around very well anymore. Courtney helps with housekeeping and cooking."

Jake's arrival had Adaline feeling as if spring had sprung. She wasn't sure why she'd taken such a shine to him. Maybe because so much time had passed since she felt a sense of peace about anything. Her mother died when her sister was only three and she'd been five. Then her father had always had a difficult time keeping a job. And a year ago, Dr. Black gave them the bad news, and nothing was the same.

Since then, Courtney had been a handful. Adaline loved her little sister, but they didn't see eye to eye on everything. Well, actually, on very little.

Mrs. Torry appeared in the doorway. "Mr. Costner, Adaline's room is made up with clean sheets like you asked. Will your son be staying for supper?"

Jake's gaze flicked between her father and Mrs. Torry as if he was surprised. Perhaps he'd planned to stay in town.

"Of course he is, Mrs. Torry," Adaline answered, wanting Jake to feel welcome. "He'll be living here for as long as he likes." She glanced at her father, who nodded his agreement.

"I guess that's up to what Jake wants," he said. "As much as we'd like him to stay, we can't force him."

Jake and their father exchanged a glance. She could tell Jake hadn't forgiven him for his betrayal. And why should he?

Adaline had been shocked to learn she had a half brother, one her father had never mentioned before two months ago. She still couldn't believe her father, who'd been a loving, doting man his whole life, had kept such a secret. Had her mother known? Adaline didn't think so, but then, she'd been quite young when her mother had passed away.

Another surge of protectiveness welled up. She felt Jake's pain. Wondered how she would have fared if the tables had been turned. That was something she didn't like to contemplate.

Chapter Five

Before supper, Jake followed the detailed directions Adaline had given to the livery where he planned to stable his horse. As he led Joker along in the cool evening air, he fingered the handful of coins in his pocket, thinking in a short time he'd put a dent into the amount of money he'd brought along. He'd best be frugal when he could. No telling how long he'd be in Newport.

His friend Dalton Babcock was never far from his mind. Was that really him? If Jake didn't find out what was going on and do something soon, he might lose his chance. Sending a telegram to Albert would alert the telegraph operator to his suspicions—and maybe open a can of worms that could get him into trouble. No telling whom he could trust.

No, this was something he'd have to do on his own if he didn't want to end up aboard a ship to Alaska himself.

Was there a way he could get close enough to Dalton to be sure of his identity? Still, he'd never believe Dalton was guilty of murder. Had his friend gotten mixed up in some bad business in San Francisco, where the crime was being in the wrong place at the wrong time?

Jake turned the corner into the main part of the town, the brackish sea air heavy on his skin. Oregon was so different from Wyoming—and Nebraska, he presumed.

Could I ever live here? What would make a man leave home? Why had his father seen Newport as a better place than being with his mother? Because of the greener grass, the endless blue of the ocean? Or maybe the reason was once he arrived here, he had no place farther to go? Was his father just running away?

Adaline had said tourists came from the Willamette Valley, as well as all over the world, to see the ocean here, dig in the famous oyster beds, and eat clams.

Jake twisted his lips, remembering the distasteful flavor the shelled creatures had left in his mouth. As far as he was concerned, the Oregonians could keep the shellfish they were so proud of. Give him a slow-roasted prairie hen, or a thick slice of elk, hot off the fire. When the day arrived to go home, he wouldn't hesitate.

He turned, the road now leading west. A breathtaking view halted his feet. The sun descending into the sea shimmered like magic, and the water below reflected pink and golden clouds. He'd never seen the likes. A gust of wind pushed back his hair and the call of a night bird rent the air.

The Wind River Range came to mind, with its towering mountains, wide canyons, rushing rivers, and silent meadows. Whenever he was there, he felt he'd entered a realm not found on earth. But *this* sunset was unlike anything he'd ever experienced.

How he wished Daisy was here to see the display. His heart wasn't in Oregon—*now*—but maybe if a person stayed long enough . . .

Just ahead, the livery was dark and quiet. But so was the other road leading to where he'd disembarked the train. And just down the track from the depot would be the prison camp, where the man he believed to be Dalton awaited his awful fate.

What could Jake find out? And how? Without getting closer, making a determination would be impossible.

I could be wrong. Maybe the prisoner's not Dalton. That would sure make life easier.

An image of a broken-down miner happening into the Bright Nugget in Logan Meadows some time back came to mind. The fellow's ragged clothes were filthy and hung from his skeletal frame. Without any teeth, his lips rolled inward, and he spoke with a lisp. He'd begged a drink from Kendall, the saloon owner, and only after the whiskey had warmed his sunken belly had shared the horrors of his days spent working a mine in Juneau, Alaska. Supplies were scarce, and the weather bitter cold. The darkness throughout the winter and far into the summer had depressed all their spirits. The fella had dreamed of someday making it home to Texas, and was headed there then. The next day, Albert had found him dead in the alley behind the saloon, his eyes open and a hand stretched out.

Was the tall prisoner really Dalton? How much worse would a prison camp be? Jake wouldn't stick his nose in without making sure.

In the fading light, he turned from the livery and ambled down the middle of the dirt road, not drawing a look from anyone. People must be used to tourists showing up. He passed a hardware store where a man was turning his sign to CLOSED, and a restaurant where something cooking actually smelled good. From a saloon up ahead, laughter and shouts reverberated.

A second later, two men burst from the door, carrying on about something.

Jake recognized one as a guard from the prison camp and quickly turned away.

Hope blossomed. Had this one gotten off duty, relieved by someone else? Or did they sometimes leave the place with only one guard?

One way to know for sure. Continuing on, Jake reached the depot within moments. He saw a man inside the dim interior. He turned, leading his horse toward the place where he'd received Joker off the train.

With the sun down past the far horizon, the shadows disappeared and light faded. All the dark grays and browns of these coastal lands made perception difficult. For a good minute, his horse's footfalls were the only sound. Then a flicker of a campfire came into view. He slowly crept closer.

"You!" a deep voice called out. "Stop!"

Jake turned. The guard he'd seen at the saloon followed behind, a wooden box in his arms. His shirttail hung out and a rip marred his sleeve. When he was within five feet, he stopped. Plates of food were stacked inside the crate, along with a few loaves of bread.

"What's your business out here?"

Jake toed the earth in front of his boot, stalling for time. He recalled something Sarah, Chase and Jessie's young daughter, had told the family at the dinner table the night of his going-away supper. She'd spoken in great detail of a school assignment about old bones.

"I'm hunting for . . . fossils, bones and such."

"What the devil you say?" The man's gaze jerked around as if giant rattlesnakes were lying in wait. "What's a fossil?"

Joker nudged Jake with his nose. "You know what a fossil is. It's, uh, the remains or impression of some kind of animal or plant from thousands of years ago."

Enough light remained to see the man's eyes narrow. He wasn't buying it. Thing was, Jake needed to get a little closer to the camp. A man with Dalton's build had just ambled outside the train car and was watching them.

"A thousand years ago? I never heard of nothin' like that. You're lying." The guard set the box on the ground and palmed the handle of his holstered revolver.

Jake pointed to the ground. "I'm not. Seems there was once these gigantic creatures called Dinosauria living in this area." *At least in Wyoming Territory.* "Some were larger than the hotel I saw in town. I'm a bone hunter. Finding something old is worth *a lot* of money." *What else did Sarah say? Something about fish fossils?*

"You don't look like nothin' but a saddle tramp. Where's your—" The man glanced at Joker. "Your equipment? You must need something to find these Dinosauria."

Emboldened, Jake took another two steps toward the enclosure. The man he thought was Dalton still watched their approach.

"Nope, just my eyes and my hands. The fossils can be fish too. Pressed onto a rock or ... or shale." He shrugged. "Especially around the ocean." He hunkered down and fingered the sandy loam. "This area is rich in 'em. If I were you, I'd keep my eyes open. Could be worth money."

Jake noticed a thick stick a good ten feet closer to the wire enclosure. Without asking, he pointed and then boldly walked forward.

He was near enough now. Jake had only seen those caramel-colored eyes on one man. He hoped his friend didn't call out if he recognized him. This guard looked plenty skeptical already.

"Hold up," the guard commanded. "Unless you want to taste my bullet."

"For what? Picking up a—" He bent, feeling sweat break out on his forehead. "Stick? There ain't no crime in that." He shook his head and gave the stick a toss. "Can't be sure in this light."

As certain as he could be about Dalton without actually speaking with him, Jake wondered if Dalton recognized him from Logan Meadows and made the connection. Jake still didn't know what he was going to do, only that something was drastically wrong.

It's no mistake—Dalton Babcock is about to be shipped off to Alaska, and I'm the only one who can help him.

<hr />

Darkness weaved in and out, making reality and dreams undistinguishable. Pain throbbed in his head, and then burned down his spine. With little strength—and less volition, he lay in the bed of straw, thinking about lifting an arm to find the source of his discomfort.

The air around him reeked sharp and salty and caught in the back of his throat. He fisted a hand when the floor pitched up, then rolled gently back, making his stomach pinch. The shrill cry of a gull pierced his agony. He thought he might have vomited somewhere along the way, but couldn't be sure.

A ship?

Was he out to sea?

Someone from across the darkness moaned in anguish. What had happened? Where was he? He tried to gather his thoughts, but a weighty fog of ambiguity pulled him deeper and deeper into confusion until he allowed the sleep wafting at the back of his forehead greater admittance.

With an anguished cry, he sat up, panic making his heart race. The dream—no, nightmare, that haunted him whenever he closed his eyes—had returned. Weak and unsteady, he rolled to his knees to climb to his feet and ventured out into the cool evening air.

The hazy ground seemed to come and go before his eyes. Red ants scurrying over his boots were hypnotic, giving him a feeling of peace and euphoria. Just like in the dream, his head throbbed, but he resisted the urge to reach up and feel the knot under his hat. The last time he had, one of the keepers had yelled so loudly, the sound had almost knocked him off the bench where he sat. If he remained still and quiet, he could make it through one more hour. Then maybe the keepers would give him some bread.

His friend, Number Four, had made a fuss yesterday, calling to some men on the outside standing by the train. Before the prisoner had been able to say much, the keepers had shot him dead, said he was trying to escape. He'd never seen a Number Two. Perhaps that fellow died on their way here, wherever here was.

With great effort, he raised his face to the darkening sky and watched a large white gull lift up and float across the expanse of slate, free on the wind. The bird became smaller and smaller until only a speck remained.

If only the jumbled nonsense in his head would stop, he could make sense of his surroundings. Where was he? He had to stay alert. Was something wrong with the food? After the meals was when his thoughts became jumpy, and staying awake became even more difficult.

With heavy-lidded eyes, he gazed at the bench and contemplated the effort needed to sit. Soon it would be time to eat. Movement on the road by the railroad caught his eye. Yes, sustenance was on its way.

Chapter Six

By the time Courtney arrived home at half past seven, Adaline was more than worried something terrible had happened. The back door opened slowly as her sister tried to sneak in. Courtney's hair, a tangled mess, left little doubt in Adaline's mind where she'd been.

Because of Jake's arrival, they'd held supper for Courtney so they could all eat together. Poor Mrs. Torry was distraught everything she'd prepared had become dry and tasteless.

"Where've you been?" Adaline demanded, struggling to hold back her temper. By the looks of Courtney's rumpled clothes and hair, her shenanigans were quite evident. "Let me guess. Spending time with Wil? You know Papa asked you not to see him anymore. He's much too old for you. Jake arrived today and because of you, the supper Mrs. Torry has so generously fixed will be put on the table cold, or close to it. What do you have to say for yourself?"

"What I do is none of your concern," Courtney said. Her eyes softened. "How's Papa?"

True to form, Courtney was changing the subject.

"The same. If you'd come home on time, you'd know that."

Courtney tried to walk past. "Again, I'm not your con—"

"You *are* my concern, Courtney." Adaline caught her sister's arm. "Wil's no good. His kind only has one thing in mind—and it's not preserving your reputation. I'm begging you to use your head before you ruin your life."

At the raised voices, she wasn't surprised when Jake stepped into the kitchen. He'd returned from taking his horse into town thirty minutes ago and had been washing up in his room.

"How do you know so much about men? You've never had a beau," Courtney responded, casting a curious look at Jake. To his credit, he didn't flinch at her frown.

"If you want to play dumb, that's your choice," Adaline shot back, gesturing to the set table. "At least hurry yourself. We've been waiting for over a half hour."

With a flip of her hair, Courtney stepped into her room and closed her door none too gently.

Embarrassed for her outburst, Adaline glanced at Jake. She no longer had to shoulder her younger sister's rebellious behavior alone. The feeling was nice.

"Courtney?" he asked.

Adaline nodded. "I'm sorry for the scene your first night here," she said, wondering what he was thinking. "Courtney wasn't always unmanageable and angry. She became withdrawn after Papa's diagnosis. Then she met Wil Lemon. The man fills her head with defiance. She's now outspoken and insolent—and I know her behavior is because of him. She pushes her boundaries at every turn. Since I'm only two years older, I'm not much of an authority figure. She'll be out of school soon, and I don't like to think about what she'll do with all her extra time."

"Work?"

"Yes, at least I hope so." She glanced at Courtney's closed bedroom door, a room that Adaline now shared with her sister, wishing she could rewind the scene and handle everything differently, use more restraint and love. "I'm glad you're here, Jake."

A ghost of a smile pulled up the corners of his mouth. "Safety in numbers?"

She had to laugh. "Yes, something like that."

Courtney's bedroom door opened. She went to the table, followed by Jake and Adaline. Mrs. Torry already had everything there. They served in silence and then Adaline offered a brief blessing.

"Does your father ever come downstairs to eat?" Jake asked, taking the platter of salmon, all the while eyeing the flaky pink fish. He scooped a portion.

"Your father too." Adaline took the platter as he passed it. "And no, not for about a month. He's much too weak. One of us usually sits with him and helps. Tonight, since you're here, Mrs. Torry has offered so we can get a chance to become acquainted." She smiled when he eyeballed his plate one more time, taking a small sniff. "Have you ever had Pacific salmon before?"

Jake shook his head. "I've never had any seafood until earlier today. I can't say I loved the oysters from your local restaurant." He lifted a sliver of salmon on his fork and put it in his mouth.

"No?" Adaline asked.

Courtney laughed. "You act like salmon is something strange. It's fish. You've had fish, I'm sure."

Jake swallowed, a small smile appearing. "Oh, sure. Cutthroat trout, catfish, turtle sometimes. You come out to Wyoming and I'll fry you up some grizzly bear bacon or mountain oysters. We'll see how much you like those," he said to Courtney.

"Mountain oysters?" she asked. "Then this isn't your first try with seafood. Stop acting like our food is so different from what you're used to."

"When you're older, little sister," he said with affection, "I'll tell you what mountain oysters are. Here's a hint—they don't come from the ocean."

Adaline looked at him in confusion, wondering why they had to wait.

"I noticed a small yard with prisoners," Jake said, changing the subject. "We have jails and penitentiaries where I'm from, but nothing like the camp sitting down by the tracks."

"We call the place the convict yard," Courtney said. "When did you see it? It's pretty well tucked out of sight."

"When I was unloading my horse from the train."

She leaned forward, her eyes wide. "Your horse?"

"That's right. I wouldn't have brought him if I'd known you lived in town."

"Can I see him sometime?" she asked.

"Sure. He's in the livery if you want to take him out. He's gentle if you know how to ride." Jake reached for his water glass and took a drink.

Courtney's eyes brightened. "I do."

"Not well," Adaline said, correcting her. "If you go, make sure Jake's with you."

"Can we do that, Jake?"

"Just let me know when. Is there a sheriff in Newport? Any kind of lawman?"

Courtney raised a brow. "You're just full of interesting questions, aren't you? I can't imagine why you'd want to know that."

"And you're being rude, Courtney," Adaline replied sternly, making Courtney smile. "Watch your manners." She glanced at Jake.

"Nope, no sheriff." Courtney laughed playfully. "We have a traveling judge who comes through, but haven't had a sheriff since the last man to wear a star was killed—about six months ago. He was the third in a row. Seems no one wants the job now. Why do you ask?"

"I didn't see a jail when I walked to the livery. Just wondered."

Adaline took a bite of her rice and again wiped her mouth with her napkin. "The two-story building is located on the next street over. A man named Lee Strangely thinks he's a lawman. Sits in the office all day and sees to easy issues. He's part of the Army unit that watches over the convicts before they're shipped out on the boat." Frowning, she added, "I'd feel better if someone would accept the sheriff position—but I understand why they don't. The local businessmen run the show around here, and some of them I don't trust."

"Adaline, how can you say that? You've lived here all your life. They're our friends."

"It's how I feel."

Courtney turned to Jake, a mischievous glint in her eyes. "Why don't you be our sheriff? As Adaline said, the town could use you. You look like a Western cowboy-sheriff type, right out of the pages of a book."

"Courtney!"

Jake laughed and pushed back in his chair. "Settle down, Adaline, she's just playing. I'm only here long enough to get a few answers from your father, and I'll be headed back to Logan Meadows. That's where I belong."

Disappointment moved inside. Now that Adaline had found her brother, she didn't want to lose him.

"Your father too, Jake," she said softly. "I wouldn't let you be sheriff even if you wanted to. Not with how fast the last one was killed."

"Was he murdered?"

She nodded. "Since we don't have a sheriff to look into the case, follow up on leads, no one ever found out who did it, or why. It's unnerving. Same for the other two. Stands to reason, a murderer lives among us."

Jake tipped his head. "I don't like the sound of that. Didn't know Oregon had this much lawlessness. Where I'm from, good people take care of each other. We try not to let murderers roam free, even if Newport is three times the size of Logan Meadows."

Finished, Courtney laid her fork and knife across her plate. "Just because we're on the coast doesn't mean we're not out west. The Wyoming Territory isn't the only place with outlaws and thieves."

"I guess you're right," he said.

Courtney nodded. "No guessing to it."

"Why hasn't anyone sent for a federal marshal? To get to the bottom of the murders?"

"That's a very good question," Adaline said. "And the exact one I put to Mr. Strangely. He says the Army is seeing to the matter. I think he doesn't want a marshal snooping around."

The look Jake gave her was supposed to be calming, she was sure, but his expression had the precise opposite effect. She and her brother were cut from the same cloth. He liked all the unanswered questions about as much as she did.

Was there any possibility he might change his mind about returning to Wyoming? Could she make that happen?

Chapter Seven

Jake strode away from the house in the unwelcoming Oregon air—damp and chilly—and retraced his steps toward town. Without a lawman to speak with, getting access to Dalton Babcock was nearly impossible.

Knowing time was of the essence once they'd said good night to Costner and turned in, he'd lain atop the bed, waiting for everyone in the house to fall asleep. Finally, after midnight, he'd pulled on his dark rain slicker for cover and, with hat in hand, crept out into the kitchen and then out the back door.

Except for noise from the tavern, the streets were quiet. Every few minutes, the deep *clang-clang-clang* of a very large bell sounded through the whispery white mist hugging the ground. Adaline had spoken at dinner about the lighthouse in Yaquina Bay, and now he was experiencing it firsthand.

He paused and looked around. Home was as different from this damp seaside town as night was to day. Deciding to try a different route, he passed the street that turned by the livery he'd taken to the prison yard before, and continued on. When he thought he'd gone far enough, he ducked between two buildings and was about to cross an open expanse when he heard a noise behind him.

Have I been seen? Am I being followed?

The name Lee Strangely kept rolling around in his mind. Jake would have a difficult time explaining what he was doing out here in the dead of night. His simple bone-hunter explanation probably wouldn't hold water.

Pressing himself next to the building, he waited.

Anger ripped through Jake when he recognized the outline of Adaline following in his footsteps, wearing a long coat and with a scarf over her head.

"What're you doing?" he gritted through clenched teeth. This was dangerous. He might explain away his reason for being out after midnight lurking around town, but not his sister's.

"That's the question I want to ask you," she shot back, not the least bit intimidated by his tone when he stepped from the shadows.

"I know the squeak of my bedroom door," she said. "When I realized you hadn't just gone to the kitchen for some water, I was curious, and then worried. Thought you meant to check on your horse, but now I see you have something else in mind. What are you up to, Jake? Now your innocent questions at supper make sense. Don't you dare lie."

Jake jumped forward and pressed his hand over her mouth. "Shh," he whispered close to her ear. "Someone's coming." He pulled her none too gently to the side of the building, and they both flattened themselves against the bricks.

The last thing he wanted was to get Adaline mixed up in what he had planned. She could be hurt ... or killed. From the discussion at the supper table, this town didn't leave much room for mistakes.

In a moonbeam cutting through the fog, a silhouette appeared plainly visible in the mouth of the alley. The man, at least six foot three, stopped and then looked around.

Jake's heart wedged in his throat, and he held his breath. *Don't come down this way.*

Adaline reached out silently and touched his hand.

After a moment more, the man moved on. Jake breathed out in relief and heard Adaline do the same.

She grasped his arm but stayed up against the wall. "What is this about, Jake? Are you an outlaw, here to rob the bank? Are you in some sort of trouble you're not saying?"

If they hadn't just had such a close call, he would have laughed. "No, of course not. I'm here to meet my father, and now the sisters I never knew I had."

"Then why are you sneaking around in the dark, and asking us about a sheriff and everything else. I want to know." When the wind threatened to take her scarf, she reached up and pulled the material around her face. "I'm not taking another step until you tell me, Jake, so just forget about anything you're thinking now."

Yeah, they pretty much thought alike—a family trait?

"Level with me."

"Keep your voice down," he demanded. "I'll tell you. When I was unloading my horse from the train, one of the convicts caught my attention. He looks like a fella I know. Came to Logan Meadows some six months back, and now resides in San Francisco. He's a good man, not an outlaw. Right before my trip here, our sheriff received a letter from him, saying he was headed back to Logan Meadows. Now he's dressed in black stripes and bound for Alaska? Something doesn't add up. His incarceration happened too fast. I can't in good conscience just turn a blind eye. Something is wrong, and I aim to find out."

"You aim to break him out?"

"Maybe."

"Jake, you'll never get away with it. You'll be killed!"

The fear in her voice told him just how much she'd come to care in the short time they'd been acquainted. Deeply touched by the thought, he realized how pleased he was to have met her.

"The cemetery is full of bodies of unfortunate men having something to do with that horrible place. I'm begging you to reconsider. Leave this alone. Maybe this friend of yours is guilty? You have no idea what they're—"

"Thought I saw someone turn down this alley," a voice boomed out.

Stupid. The man had circled around and come at them from the other direction, and Jake hadn't suspected a thing. He was close enough now Jake recognized the tattered uniform of the guards, and was relatively sure the sentinel wasn't the same one who had questioned him earlier. Jake grasped Adaline and pulled her to his chest in a lover's shielding move, causing her to gasp in surprise.

"Mind your own business," Jake responded tersely. They were far enough away from the convicts' camp that their visitor shouldn't be suspicious of their true motive.

The man took a large step forward, his face twisted. "What did you just say?"

Jake stepped up too, pushing Adaline behind him and moving his coat away from his gun in a threatening manner. "I said—get outta here. Can't a man have a little time with his gal? If I hear you say no, I'm bound to get mighty irritated. Things were just heating up."

He wasn't sure yet what he would do, but whatever the decision, there'd be a fight. One that would draw the attention of the earlier guard who would recognize him instantly.

The man chuckled. "I guess there ain't no law against sparkin'."

"Didn't think so." Jake straightened, not wanting to show any sign of fear or weakness. "I'm waitin' to see your backside moving away."

"Don't push your luck." The guard turned and headed back to the enclosure where he'd most likely stand watch all night.

"That was close," Adaline said, still standing behind him.

"Yeah, too close. That's why I don't want you involved. It's dangerous."

"Please, Jake, drop this foolishness."

He thought of Daisy, and how he would let her down if he never came home. His muscles tensed at the thought. "I can't."

"Is this worth getting killed over?"

Now she was being a burr under his saddle. "There's a code between men. If I don't live up to it, I won't be able to look at myself in the mirror. He's a friend, Adaline. I can't pretend I never saw him. What if the tables were turned? I'd sure want his help."

Her brow remained crimped.

"Let's just say I wouldn't be much of a man if I didn't at least try."

Adaline glanced down the alley and rubbed her hands up and down her arms. The clanging of the fog bell sounded, and she looked up at Jake and smiled. "No, I guess you wouldn't. And neither would I."

"What? Be a man?"

She laughed and slapped his arm. "You know what I mean. I'm helping. You can't do this alone."

"That's crazy."

"That's the truth."

Chapter Eight

Mrs. Torry glanced up from whatever she was cooking on the stove when Jake returned from his early morning visit to the telegraph office. He'd sent a telegram to Daisy and one to the ranch, to let them know he'd arrived in time to meet his father.

The housekeeper gave him a curt nod. Not seeing anyone else about, Jake wandered into the dining room where they'd taken supper last night and looked around, marveling at the astonishing fact he'd learned yesterday.

He had sisters. Two of them. A detail he hadn't shared in his messages. He needed to know more, get his feet set firmly on solid ground. Only a week ago, he was shocked to learn he had a father who wanted to meet him, and now this . . .

Jake went back into the kitchen. "Is Mr. Costner awake?"

"He is. Said you were to come up whenever you wanted. He's had his coffee, and breakfast won't be ready for a while. You have time to go up for a visit before these potatoes are done."

Jake poured himself a cup of coffee, still feeling somewhat of an intruder, and headed for the stairs. He paused at the open door to see if Costner was still awake. The man was no more than a small lump under the covers. One of the windows was open slightly, giving vital fresh air to the deep heaviness of the room.

Would today be the day? He wished he could feel something for the man, as he did already for his sisters, but whenever he tried, a deep, dark, uncrossable gorge opened between them.

Costner looked up and waved Jake inside. "Son, please, come sit with me," he wheezed. "I'd like to talk."

That Costner so easily called him son irked Jake. As if they'd been one big happy family all these years. As if they counted on each other, went hunting, and discussed what and who was best for the girls. Jake took the chair, so familiar now, even after only one day.

"How are you, Jake? Did you sleep well?"

The man looked different. Weaker. Jake braced his feelings, taking a drink from his coffee cup. "I slept fine," he fibbed. "Just trying to make sense out of all this."

The nod was almost imperceptible. "I know. Life can startle the stuffing out of you. Tell me about yourself, Jake. You'd said you live in Logan Meadows. I've not heard of the place before. What's the town like? Just like a good poker player, you've kept your cards close to your chest. I understand that, I do. But now, will you indulge me a little? We don't have much time. I'd like us to get to know each other." He smiled and gazed into Jake's eyes. "Are you married?"

How could he deny a dying man? One who was his father? He couldn't and wouldn't. But that didn't mean he had to forgive him. He'd tell Costner what he wanted to know, but he didn't have to excuse his father's abandonment.

"No, not married yet, but I have a special girl."

Costner nodded and smiled. "What's her name?"

"Daisy Smith."

"Nice name. What's she look like? How old is she?"

The memory of Daisy's light brown hair made Jake's fingers tingle. He thought of their parting, and of her lips against his. She was always the prettiest girl in the room, and had a way of making his heart skip a beat with just a smile.

"Jake? Is that too personal?"

"No." He shook his head. "Daisy's real pretty. She has brown hair the color of chestnuts streaked with sunshine and pretty green eyes. She's the same age as Adaline."

"You have plans to marry?"

Jake nodded.

"Do it, son, as soon as you get back. Don't wait. Life is short. When you're young, you think you have all the time in the world to do all the things you want. Grand things and small things. This, that, and another. The only things I think about now are my wife and daughters. My parents. And now you. I even think of Marlene. People are what matter. All the rest is just leaves in the wind."

Without the girls here, his father's strong demeanor had fizzled away. He gave a weak cough without the energy to lift his hand.

Jake reached forward and plumped the extra pillow behind his back, propping him up. He found the handkerchief lost in the bed linen and wiped his father's lips, and then put the cloth in his grasp.

"Thank you."

God. Why this? Why now? I can't feel sorry for him. Not after what he did to my mother. He knew where I was my entire life, but never wanted to meet me. Why should I care about him? Chase and Jessie have been my parents in the real way. Am I being disloyal to them to feel this empathy now? For this stranger who has sired me?

Costner's eyes brightened for a moment before they faded back into his face. "I have some issues I'd like to speak about.

Before the girls come up." His Adam's apple bobbed, and his gaze moved to his water.

Jake brought the glass over and helped him drink.

"I know I wronged you, Jake. Your mother too. In a horribly bad way. Thinking about it disgusts me. But there isn't a thing I can do to make things better. If I could go back and change the situation, I would. I promise you that. I wouldn't have taken from her what was never mine to have. I wouldn't have led her on, letting her think I was staying." His head wobbled on the pillow. "So many things I could have done better. I don't have anything of real value to pass on, son. I wish I did. I've been borrowing against the house for years and finally lost it to the bank. The banker's a good fellow. Rents the place to me cheap."

Costner's breathing picked up for a few moments, bringing a spurt of fear to Jake. His chest jerked, and then he coughed. After a large intake of breath, his breathing went back to normal.

"I'm sure you know now why I bade you here. You're a smart fellow, and I have nothing to hide. As much as I've wanted to meet you over the years, I could have at any time. Son, I didn't want to ruin your life. At least if you didn't know me, you could pretend about your pa, make up grand ideas that he was some important person, like a rancher or politician. I've been a nobody all my life. A clerk here, a helper there. If not for my wife's money, I'd never have owned a house. In my own way, I've loved you. Thought of you, dreamed of you. After meeting you, I realize how erroneous I was. But now, with my dying, I had no choice."

Jake felt his eyes well. He wouldn't cry. He called to mind the last time he'd allowed himself. He'd been five or six, out wandering the streets late into the night, hunger burning in his belly and deep pain beleaguering his heart. The stars had been so bright, he'd pretended if he closed his eyes and believed hard enough, he could transport himself away, up into the sky. Where someone would want him. Love him. When the stars wavered and he felt hot tears scald his cheeks, he'd lain down in the grass and cried until he didn't have any more tears.

"Adaline and Courtney need you, Jake. I don't want to leave them all alone. They have no relatives that I know of on their mother's side. Courtney is only fifteen and already has a grown man thinking things he shouldn't. Wil Lemon is rough and mean. Has a bad reputation around town. If they married, I fear what would become of her. I don't dare forbid her, or she'll run to him all the faster. That's her nature."

Costner coughed again before continuing. "The girls haven't had an easy life. They may be painting a pretty picture for you now, but believe me, they've had their share of sorrow—and of scraping by. They'll need you, Jake. I'm praying you'll take them with you when you go. Take them to your town, to Logan Meadows, and be a family. Will you do that? Not for me. For them." His hands gripped the blanket so tightly, his knuckles were white.

His pleading tone burned at Jake.

"For you too. I'm begging you, son, tell me you won't let them down."

Chapter Nine

Adaline and Courtney returning with him to Logan Meadows?

"Jake? Say something. I think my time is here—now. I don't have much longer. Are you thinking of going to Michigan? To find our people? My parents, if they're still alive, will be delighted to know I had a son to carry on the Costner name. You look so much like I used to, they won't have a problem believing you're mine." His gaze shot to the bedside table and he reached out for the drawer, but a rough round of coughing stalled his hand.

Jake opened the drawer.

"Hand me the paper and pencil," his father wheezed out. "I'll write a note. Date it. Put some details only I could know. They're good Christians, and I doubt you'd need to use this, but just in case. You'll like them, Jake. If your grandfather *has* passed, I'm sure my uncle will let you take up in the family business where I was supposed to be. Do it, if you want."

A spark of determined fire shone in Costner's eyes, his tone desperate. "Just promise to take Adaline and Courtney with you wherever you go. I can see in their expressions they're frightened. The three of you are a family now, and you're the head of the household."

He shrugged his frail shoulders. Exhausted from all the talking, his hand stopped mid-sentence. He closed his eyes briefly before continuing. "Always have been, I guess. Maybe going east would be the best for you all."

Jake wasn't going anywhere except back to Logan Meadows. Maybe later he'd make the trip to Michigan to meet his family, but not now. Until then, he could reach out in a letter and see what their reception would be. For now, Daisy was waiting on him, and he wouldn't let her down.

Sounds of the girls coming up the stairs made Costner's eyes go wide. With a shaky hand, he signed the note, folded the missive, and handed it over. "Jake?"

"You've nothing to worry about. No one's looking after my sisters except me. I promise you that."

"Papa?" Adaline's voice preceded her.

A moment later, both she and Courtney appeared in the doorway, still wearing their housecoats and wool socks pulled up to their knees. Both blondes, Adaline's hair was longer and fell to the middle of her back, where Courtney's was just past her shoulders. Their eyes were identical, a soft blue with an abundance of lashes. Where Adaline was slender and graceful, Courtney looked athletic and strong—a girl he might see wrangling a steer. The mental image brought a smile.

"How do you feel, Papa?" Courtney asked.

Costner might think both girls would happily go along with whatever Jake said, but he had his doubts about the youngest. She seemed to have a mind of her own, her thoughts always somewhere else. The only thing Courtney liked about him was Joker, his horse. Adaline was another story entirely.

Their father patted the bed. "Sit and visit a while, both of you. We have a lot to talk about." His gaze went to Jake's, and he smiled.

Adaline did as her father asked, circled the bed and climbed up. The love in her eyes was easy to see. "Only a moment, Papa. I don't want to be late to work."

Courtney rolled her eyes. "No, you wouldn't. Mrs. Bennett can be a fright. She gets upset over everything. I don't know how you stand working in the mercantile with her breathing down your neck."

"She's not that bad," Adaline replied.

"And you're off to school," Costner said, his attention on his youngest.

"Not today. I've worked ahead, and Mrs. Knight said I can have the day off."

If Jake wasn't mistaken, her chin edged up, as if preparing for a fight.

"Wil's coming by in a little while," she hurried on. "He's taking me for a buggy ride, and then we'll get a bite to eat at the café. You don't mind, do you?"

"No school? That doesn't seem right."

Courtney huffed. "I'm the brightest in the class now that Adaline is gone. You remember how Mrs. Knight let Adaline off when she'd worked ahead, don't you?" She glanced at her sister, who just held her gaze without saying anything.

Costner nodded, even though Jake could tell he was skeptical. "You know how I feel about Wil Lemon, and you stepping out with him. Why don't—"

"We're *not* courting, Papa." She laughed, moved forward, and picked up her father's hand. "We're just friends. That's all. I'm like a little sister to him."

Costner frowned. "That's about right, with your age difference. He's too old for you."

She straightened, her mouth taking on a defiant slant. "Nine years isn't much difference. Mrs. Knight, our teacher, is twenty-five years younger than Mr. Knight."

"They met and married when she was thirty and he was fifty-five. A far cry from fifteen and twenty-five." His lips pressed together. "Your age difference troubles me."

"Like I said, we're just friends, so the age difference doesn't matter at all." Courtney offered him his water.

Jake watched as his father gulped down a swallow—just to please her, he was sure. Seemed his little sister had her pa wrapped around her finger good and tight.

"What about a chaperone? You can't be riding around in a buggy alone," Costner said, looking over to Jake.

A steely expression pulled his father's brows into a deep *V*, and he began to cough. The spasm began slowly, but seeing Costner could hardly catch his breath, Jake stood and helped him sit forward. Costner covered his mouth with his handkerchief, but when he pulled the cloth away, it was bright with a large splotch of blood.

Adaline gave a small cry of distress and hurried around the bed to help Jake. As did Courtney.

Finally resting again on the pillows, Costner tracked his gaze back to his youngest. "Courtney?"

"You worry too much, Papa. Do you think I'd ruin my reputation? Especially with a rascal like Wil?" She took her father's comb from his bedside table and gently, lovingly, combed back his mussed hair drooping in his face. "Wil's sister is coming along. Remember Beverly? She's twenty. Everyone in town knows her." Courtney's face actually clouded over, and tears welled in her eyes.

Jake thought she might look at him, but she didn't.

"Please let me go."

"Well, if his sister is going along too, I guess it'll be fine. Don't tarry, or you know I'll worry. Take a short ride, then go straight to the café and then home as soon as you're finished."

She leaned in and kissed his forehead. "You know I will." Courtney smiled at her sister and hurried from the room without a word, nod, or smile to Jake.

"I know no such thing," Costner mumbled, his gaze following her until she was gone. Then he looked over to the window where the wind frolicked in the trees. "No such thing at all. Courtney is headed for trouble, and she won't let me help."

Jake sat back into his chair, not a relaxed bone in his body. What would the next few days bring? More than just his father's passing, he was sure.

Chapter Ten

Sick of the stale air in the train car where he and the other man slept, Dalton shuffled out into the morning light, feeling as if someone was hammering away behind his eyes. He rubbed a shaky hand over his jaw, thick with whiskers.

Little by little, the puzzle was becoming clearer. He finally remembered his name. The man he was incarcerated with didn't look familiar. Last thing Dalton recalled before awakening here was leaving the Old Ship Saloon in San Francisco at midnight and heading to his room at the boarding house on Chestnut Street. Earlier in the evening, he thought maybe he'd eaten supper at the Cliff House before heading to the saloon.

Dalton wiped a hand across his face and stumbled to the outhouse. Afterward, he walked the perimeter of the enclosure, looking for any weak spots, an avenue of escape.

Where are the guards? This was the first time they'd left him and the other prisoner alone. They dressed like soldiers, but something in their faces, in their eyes, made him doubt.

Why was his thinking so befuddled? He reached up and fingered the good-sized lump on the back of his head. Something a few days old and shouldn't make this hazy compliance weigh all his limbs. *They must be putting something in the food.* Opium or laudanum, or some other to make him weak and confused.

"Heard 'em talkin' last night."

Dalton swung around so fast, he'd have lost his breakfast if he'd had any in his belly. "What?"

Number One, a skinny fellow about thirty-five years old, stared him in the face. His wire-rimmed glasses were mangled, and Dalton wondered how they stayed on. The lens on the left side was completely gone.

"A ship's coming for us. Taking us to Alaska. We'll be put to work in some mine, never to return." Tears welled in the small man's eyes.

That didn't sound promising. A feeling akin to fear pushed up Dalton's spine. "When?"

"Don't know. They said it was overdue."

Dalton looked through the small split in the trees to the choppy waters of the sea. He pictured a large vessel with several tall masts. Maybe once he used to like to watch the comings and goings of the boats, but he couldn't be sure. "We've been shanghaied. I've heard of the practice before. Especially in San Francisco."

The little man just stared.

The train whistle sounded before the locomotive came into sight. The black-and-silver engine emerged through a stand of coastal trees, chugging to a stop at the depot. Dalton watched the billow of steam from behind its wheels shoot up toward the sky. Folks on the decking waited as the passengers came down the steps, then when everyone else was off, they boarded.

Hope moved within. The soldiers were away.

Dalton narrowed his eyes, peering through the fog in his head, looking for any man coming their way, to the stock cars on the end of the train. Perhaps he could yell out. Attract some attention. When they came close, he would ask for their help. He searched for an opportunity but had to grasp the corner post to steady himself.

Number One, still standing next to him, grabbed hold of his arm. "Don't," he hissed, tipping his head toward the road.

One of the guards was on his way back, a box in his arms and a scowl on his face. The metal of his gun glinted in the sunlight. He was the guard who had shot the Mexican prisoner a few days earlier.

Dalton watched the guard's approach, his lip curling. He wasn't going to Alaska. There must be a way out. "What's your name?" he asked, keeping his voice low.

"Jay Merryweather, I think."

"Dalton Babcock. Don't let on you remember your name, or anything else. We don't have much time to fix this problem before our opportunity is gone."

Fear skittered across the man's face. He nodded. "I think I'm a tailor, but I'm having a difficult time putting together what happened before I ended up here. Do you know?"

The guard was close now.

"Best to keep quiet," Dalton whispered and then swayed to the side, catching the post for support once again. "Try not to eat the food," he mumbled. "I think that's how they're drugging us."

Jay's face blanched even whiter. "Why? What do they want with us?"

"Slavery. You've ended up in a pickle, Merryweather."

Dalton leaned back and looked up at the sky, scratching his chin while mumbling a long, unintelligible string of words. These fools didn't know who they were dealing with. He might not get out, but he'd die trying.

"Get over here if you want grub," the guard yelled once he arrived at the compound. With a key hanging on a chain locked around his waist, he worked the latch and opened the gate.

Dalton watched his every move like a wolf waiting to pounce. He just hoped he'd have an opportunity before all his chances were gone.

Chapter Eleven

Courtney came out of the room and walked confidently to the front window.

From his front room chair, Jake took in her soft blue dress, her glossy hair, brushed and carefully styled, and even a tinge of pink on her lips. Not enough for just anyone to notice, but someone with his background of living in a saloon could spot face paint from a mile away. He wondered where she'd gotten it.

"You sure look pretty."

Surprised, she whirled from the window. "I didn't notice you there."

Wanting to put her at ease, he smiled.

Guiltily, her hand slowly moved to her lips. Obviously pretending she had an itch, she tried to rub off some of the pink.

"I'd like to meet this friend of yours. You don't mind, do you?"

Her eyes narrowed. "Why do you want to meet Wil?"

Jake shrugged. "Just curious, I guess. When's he coming?"

Over three hours had passed since her speech in her father's room. Adaline was gone and their father asleep.

Courtney searched up the road. Her eyes strayed to the darkening sky, and her brow wrinkled. "He should be here anytime. He didn't actually say when he was coming, just sometime in the morning."

Jake stood and went to the window, standing beside her. With his new commitment to Adaline and Courtney, a warm protectiveness had begun to grow. Until Chase and Jessie took him in, he'd never been anyone's protector. Then there was Gabe, slightly younger than Jake, who'd come to live with Jessie even before she'd married Chase. He'd brought out Sarah from the New Mexico orphanage. After the wedding, Shane had been born. Even if Jake never said the sentiments aloud, he thought of the children as his siblings and would fight to the death to protect them. Then in 1881, Daisy came along. His commitment to her was everything, and he looked forward to making her his wife.

And now he had Adaline and Courtney. His sisters were an amazing discovery.

What would Daisy think when they returned? His house on Shady Creek was far too small for all of them. The structure was basically a one-room cabin only large enough for him and Daisy once they were wed, and maybe a child. When they got back to Logan Meadows, he'd have to figure out where his sisters could live.

"That him coming now?" Jake pointed to a wagon stopping at the end of the road, a good distance before the house.

"No, he said he was bringing a proper buggy."

"He has a buggy?" Jake asked, well aware of the animosity emanating from Courtney. She didn't like all the questions.

It was her turn to shake her head.

Even though the conversation wasn't exactly friendly, Jake felt they were making strides, in a strange kind of way.

After a quiet breakfast, Adaline had cleaned the kitchen and done the dishes while Courtney went back into her room to finish getting ready. She'd changed into a simply styled dress and had a thick woolen shawl tightly wrapped around her shoulders, as if she was prepared to dash out as soon as she saw Wil Lemon arrive.

Mrs. Torry ambled into the room, a soft dust cloth clutched in her hand. A scent of lemon oil followed in her wake. Jake didn't miss the woman's disapproving glance at Courtney as she went about dusting the coffee table.

"Is Mr. Costner still asleep?" he asked, just to break up the uncomfortable stillness in the dead-quiet room.

She nodded. "He is, but I expect him to awaken any time. I have a poached egg warming in the oven, if you'd like to take that up to him when he does. With his time growing short"—another disapproving glance at Courtney—"he seems to crave having his family around him. I'm glad you came when you did, Jake," she said. "I think he'd have already died if not for you."

Courtney hadn't acknowledged the woman's entrance into the room, but Jake caught a small sound of distress escape her throat at the housekeeper's words. His youngest sister wasn't as unaffected by what was transpiring around her as she'd like to pretend.

"I'm happy to help," he responded. "Just as soon as I meet Wil. He'll be showing up soon."

Courtney whirled from the window and glared. "You're not making trouble for me and Wil. I won't let you ruin everything."

The distress behind her eyes, more than her angry words, worried him. How could a simple introduction ruin a friendship? He hoped Wil Lemon hadn't already stolen her innocence.

"Never said a thing about ruinin' anything."

She turned away. Going up on tiptoe, she laid her palm on the cold glass of the window, her eyes glowing with anticipation. When a buggy pulled up outside, she waved and rushed toward the door.

Jake caught her shoulder. "Hold on. Let him come to the door for you. It's proper." He stepped around and pulled open the door just as Wil Lemon raised his fist to knock.

Courtney's suitor yanked back in surprise. The pleasant smile on his face vanished. He looked Jake up and down and then grinned without mirth. "The long-lost brother has arrived?"

Heat flashed through Jake. He cautioned himself to hold his temper.

They stood eye to eye, the new arrival a good twenty pounds heavier. Wil hadn't taken the time to clean up for this outing as Courtney had, or if he had, Jake couldn't tell. At least he'd had the manners to remove his hat from a thick head of black hair.

Jake knew instantly this man was not a match for his baby sister. He looked even older than Courtney had said. Jake didn't miss the gun strapped to his thigh.

"That's right. Arrived Monday. I'm here to see to my father's responsibilities when he can't, and one of those is my sister Courtney." He looked past Lemon's shoulder to the empty buggy and raised an eyebrow. "I was under the impression your sister was riding along as chaperone."

Lemon snorted.

Jake still held the edge of the door, blocking entrance. The missing weight of his own .45 Colt from his thigh had not gone unnoticed. "Did I say something funny?"

"Jake," Courtney said with a gasp. "You're being rude. Let Wil come inside; it's beginning to rain."

Jake didn't dare take his gaze away from Lemon. He knew his kind very well, from all the years watching his mother work the saloon. "Would you like to come in?" he asked politely. "You're not going anywhere with Courtney unchaperoned."

Even with a chaperone, I wouldn't let her out of my sight with the likes of you.

Lemon's eyes narrowed. His gaze flicked back where Jake thought Mrs. Torry must be observing the conversation, and then they traced over to Courtney. His lips quirked up in a half smile. "No, I don't think so."

"Wil," she called. The pleading in her voice almost made Jake wince.

She stepped to Jake's side and put out a hand in supplication. "Come inside and I'll bake a cake or some cookies. We can spend the afternoon here."

Lemon let his gaze wander lazily over Courtney long enough to make Jake see red.

"It's up to you, *Wil*. I don't mind. Plenty of us here to keep things lively. But if you do decide to stay, you'll leave your gun right there," he said, pointing to the table by the door that held a pink vase, a book, and a magnifying glass. "Can't imagine why you'd need your weapon on a buggy ride, but then, I'm new to town." He didn't like the vulnerability he felt in his state of unarmed weakness.

Lemon nodded and gave an amiable chuckle. He was backing down, but wasn't happy about doing so. "That sounds good, Court," he said, his hands unfastening his gun belt. He laid the weapon where Jake had instructed. "I can't remember the last time I had warm cookies with milk."

When Courtney's suitor divested himself of his sidearm, turning the leather belt to the tabletop, Jake caught sight of a handful of slashes carved on the inside. He'd felt sure a man like Wil Lemon wasn't the kind to spend a rainy day cooped up in a kitchen. What else was an unprofessed gunslinger willing to do to win the affection—*or more*—of his baby sister?

Jake would stay aware and not give the gunman a chance.

Chapter Twelve

Adaline paced back and forth in front of the mercantile counter, two bottles of laudanum she'd been stacking on the shelf forgotten in her hands. She couldn't get Jake off her mind. This foolish idea of rescuing the man in the compound had her beside herself. He didn't know how many deaths were associated with that horrible place. She wished they'd move the camp to another port town.

In the short time since Jake had arrived, she'd come to love him. Could a sentiment as strong as love grow so quickly? Or was she just grasping at straws since his arrival meant she'd have help shouldering the crushing weight of responsibility she'd felt ever since her father's diagnosis?

Sadness pushed up her throat. *Papa is dying*. His death could happen any day. The reality was still too difficult to believe. Each passing moment was a gift. She wasn't ready to let him go, and yet, she had no choice.

And what of Courtney? Even though her younger sister acted like she didn't care, Adaline knew better. Courtney was a daddy's girl—although an observer would never know it now. Her sister was on a crash course with disaster, fibbing about school and sneaking around with Wil Lemon. What should Adaline do about them? If action wasn't taken soon, irreparable damage might be the outcome. Something Courtney might regret for the rest of her life.

Adaline paused at the window, gazing at the people walking the street, her thoughts a mile away.

"What in the world has you so distraught?" Mrs. Bennett said, her head tipped to the side with curiosity. The hands that had been busy folding several sets of towels now rested on her hips. They dropped to her side and she came closer. "I've been watching you for a good five minutes, Adaline. You've carried those same two bottles of laudanum ten trips back and forth in front of the counter. I've never seen you so distracted or upset. If you're not careful, they'll drop and break. You know how expensive laudanum is."

Adaline whirled. "Yes, I do," she said, hurrying to the shelf where they kept the medicinal cures and set them in front of the other bottles, restocking the shelf. "Sorry, Mrs. Bennett."

"Your father must be worse."

She nodded. "He's getting noticeably weaker every day."

Mrs. Bennett's prized pendulum clock that had come all the way from Denmark chimed half past ten. The Pine Restaurant across the street usually sent someone over to pick up their daily supplies, and yet their box still sat in the back workroom. The walls were closing in on her. She longed to get outside where she could think more clearly.

"Do you want me to run the supplies across the street to Mr. Pine? This is the latest they've ever been picking up their order."

"I didn't even notice, but you're absolutely correct. Go ahead, if you'd like. We're not busy, and I'm sure Mr. Pine would appreciate the gesture. Once their lunch crowd hits, he'll be good and angry someone forgot to pick up the provisions." She put out a hand and stopped Adaline as she started for the back room.

"When you're finished, take a little time off. Perhaps a walk will settle your nerves. Your father's illness can't be easy. I don't want to see you back here until it's time for Freddy's tutoring."

Adaline hesitated.

"And I won't dock your pay, if that's what you're worried about. Go on now, before I change my mind."

Adaline hurried to the back room, shouldered into her coat, and then hefted the heavy wooden box filled with a few fresh tomatoes, ten ears of shriveled-looking corn left over from the end of August, a bag of flour, and a sack of rice. Mrs. Bennett held the door as Adaline breezed through. She crossed the street and entered Pine's restaurant, going directly to the kitchen, and was met by Mr. Pine's angry voice.

She stopped and set the box on the table, not wanting to interrupt. Even at eighty, the restaurant owner could dish out a tongue-lashing like no other.

The poor cook stood with his head hanging low, glancing up now and then. Brian looked like he could use some reinforcements.

"What's wrong?" she said to Mr. Pine. "Is there something I can do to help?"

Mr. Pine swung around. "Oh, Adaline, in my agitated state, I didn't hear you come in."

"I can see that. What's happened?"

"Brian forgot to tell me his brother Brant is sick and won't be in. Now I'm a man short and don't have anyone to run the food out to the different businesses I supply."

The Pine Restaurant delivers the noon meal to the convict camp. If I can prove Jake wrong, then he'll give up this dangerous notion he's gotten into his head.

"I can make the deliveries for you. Mrs. Bennett has given me a few hours off. Just tell me where they go, and I'll get busy."

Mr. Pine gave her a thoughtful look. "Your pa sure raised you right. God rest his soul when the time comes. He hasn't passed, has he?"

Adaline shook her head and tried to ignore the painful question. She pointed to the box she'd just set on the table. "There's your order from the mercantile."

He nodded his gratitude and pointed to another box on the end, already stacked with several covered plates. "Start with the army men at the compound. They don't cotton to the food being late. Don't linger. Just drop off the box and be on your way."

"I will, Mr. Pine, don't you worry. I'll go directly there and back again."

Adaline hefted the order, being sure to keep her face masked to the heaviness. With the wooden frame, it was heftier than the crates of potatoes she was used to carrying, but she'd not let on."

"You sure you can handle that?"

"It's light as a feather."

His bushy brow lifted. "I don't believe that, but you're a good girl to help out." He gave her an endearing smile. "I'll expect you back in twenty minutes, no longer."

"Any news about the ship from Alaska?"

Mr. Pine's brow wrinkled. "No, and why would you care?"

"I don't. The question just popped into my mind since I'm going to the camp. Its arrival is always the talk of the town." She was excited to do this for Jake. She'd see if she could discover anything, then get the information back to him—and also show him how clever she could be.

With aching arms, Adaline hurried down the road, not returning anyone's inquisitive glances. Probably wondering if her father had passed away. She turned at the corner, whizzed along the side of the livery approaching the bank. She kept her gaze straight ahead and her feet moving. Mr. Hexum's office window looked out on the street, and the last thing she needed today was a conversation with him. The man was becoming increasingly insistent on an answer to his proposal—or rather, a different answer than she'd already provided.

Several steps past the bank's door, she heaved a sigh of relief as she lifted the box higher in her arms. The load was growing heavier with each step she took.

"Miss Costner! Adaline, wait up!"

Drat.

The bank owner had stepped out and was hurrying her way, an agreeable smile on his face. "I saw you go by. Let me take that heavy crate."

"Oh, no, Mr. Hexum, this isn't heavy at all. I'm just helping Mr. Pine with some deliveries. I don't have time to chat." She tried to inch forward but he was now at her side and caught her arm, and none too gently.

"I insist you call me Hugh. We're old friends. Practically engaged. Keeping up this cool pretense toward me is strange."

His tone gave her pause. It held a modicum of warning. She wondered how the man succeeded in buying so much of the land and properties around Newport, when his father hadn't done the same.

"Mr. Hexum, I don't feel comfortable with that. We are not practically engaged, and we won't ever be." She looked him straight in the eye. "Now, if you'll be so kind as to let go of my arm, then I'll be on my way."

He let his arm fall to his side, and his smile flattened. "Still uppity, *Miss* Costner? You'll change your tune soon enough."

What is that *supposed to mean?* She wasn't changing her mind about marrying him. She'd best just ignore his inane comment.

"Good day, Mr. Hexum," she said, proceeding down the boardwalk once he'd released his grip.

A few minutes later, Adaline arrived at the prison compound. The two men inside the wire fence watched her approach. She wondered which was the one Jake had recognized—the smaller, shading his eyes from the sun with one hand, or the brawnier of the two, boldly watching her arrival. A sizzle of awareness whispered down her back as she cut her gaze away from the man's hawk-like stare. Her heart thumped against her breastbone, and she sneaked another look.

Two guards sat sleeping in their chairs. She'd never been this close before. No one was allowed around since the place had been built. Lee Strangely said the enclosure was to keep the townsfolk safe, but now after what Jake was thinking, she wondered. The only person who made contact with the prisoners, except the guards, was the one runner who supplied food at lunchtime. The other times, one of the guards picked up meals and supplies.

Ignoring the men inside, she walked as softly as she could, not wanting to wake the sentinels. She set the box down.

One of the guards must have sensed her presence, because he came awake with a start. "Stay where you are," he shouted, climbing to his feet.

The other guard followed suit. When they saw a woman they didn't know, they looked at each other in question. "What's that?"

As brave as she was, she couldn't stop a crackle of fear inside. "Your noontime meal."

"Where's Brant?"

"He took sick. Mr. Pine sent me."

"A woman?"

She didn't have much time. In one second, they would demand she leave. Needing to think of something quickly, she glanced over at the prisoners. The tall, strong-looking one had his arms crossed over his chest and watched her closely. Thank goodness both guards were looking in the box and not at her.

"Why not?" she said loudly, never taking her attention away from the two criminals. "Does a person have to be from Logan Meadows to be a delivery boy?"

Arms that had been crossed fell to the large prisoner's side and his eyes narrowed. The little man did nothing.

She had her confirmation.

The brute setting out the plates glanced up. "What are you babbling about, girl? That don't make sense. Now, go on and get outta here, and don't ever come back."

Turning, Adaline started away but glanced back over her shoulder. "I might have to if you want to eat. No telling when Brant will be better."

She made sure the inmate heard what she said. At the dip of his chin, she smiled. She turned and hurried toward the depot.

Adaline had wanted to prove Jake wrong so he wouldn't risk his life doing something rash. As it turned out, she'd accomplished the exact opposite of what she'd set out to do.

Chapter Thirteen

Jake opened his eyes, unsure of what had awakened him. He'd fallen asleep in the chair next to Costner's bedside. Not surprisingly, Lemon had left only an hour after his arrival, and Mrs. Torry took Courtney with her when she headed to the butcher shop. The house was quiet.

Reaching up, he massaged his stiff neck.

"Jake."

The faint plea was ragged. Looking over, Jake found his father gazing at him. He stood and closed the short distance to the bed.

"My time has come, son. I can feel it sneaking up behind me like a crouching wolf..."

Jake imagined his father as a younger man—straight, strong of arm, sharp of eye. Not what was before him now, a scarecrow swallowed up by the bed linens.

"What can I do for you?" he asked, feeling a giant hole open inside his chest. He glanced to the bedside table and the water glass. "Would you like a drink?"

James's nod was almost imperceptible.

Carefully lifting him by the shoulders, Jake held the water glass to his father's cracked lips, making sure only a small amount went in. Setting down the glass, Jake gently laid him back and adjusted the sheet. With the cloth that was never far away, he wiped moisture from his forehead.

"The girls? Are they here?"

"No. Mrs. Torry is out too. You want me to find 'em?"

"No. Better this way." His father began coughing. When he finished, he sagged back, exhausted.

Jake wiped several bloody splotches from his mouth. The dark crimson made Jake blink and wish he could break through the invisible harness keeping him in check, refusing this poor dying man the simple act of forgiveness. This was his last chance. His father was about to expire.

"You'll keep the girls?"

"I won't go back on my word."

James took a ragged breath, then coughed a bit more. "Good." He motioned to his top drawer.

Jake pulled out a piece of paper.

"It's my dying request. So the girls won't contest you when the time comes. I think Adaline will abide, but Courtney might fight. Having something in writing may help." He let out a weak cough. "Wish I'd sent for you sooner, Jake. I hope you'll forgive me someday for waiting—and everything else. Getting to know you has been pure pleasure. Speaking with you." He managed a smile. "My son."

Jake swallowed. Pulled his gaze away.

"A son like you makes a man proud. I'm glad to know our name will live on through your children. Have a lot of young'uns, Jake. You and Daisy. Love your wife. Be thankful for every minute you have."

"I'm nothin' but a cowhand."

As he said the words, he knew they weren't really true. Maybe a few years ago, but not now. Not after what Chase and

Jessie had instilled in him. He was part of their family. They had given him siblings in Gabe, Sarah, and Shane. His life had changed again when Daisy came along. She loved him for who he was, not for his name, or what he did or didn't own. They were a team. Together, they'd create something wonderful in this wide, wondering world, and nothing would stop them.

"You're much more than that to me . . ."

That statement cut like a razor. Watching a father die wasn't an easy thing to do—regardless of what the child thought of him.

James slowly closed his eyes. A minute passed, and then another.

Leaning close, Jake tried to see any movement in the silence of the room.

"I'm still here." There was a hint of humor in his father's tone.

Nervous relief made Jake smile. He swallowed, feeling the back of his throat rub the front.

"You believe in God, Jake? I mean, do you have faith in the hereafter?"

In Sunday school, Mrs. Hollyhock had preached a blue streak, hoping the children learned their Bible verses. But not until he was alone at night, out minding the herd under a sky of glittering stars, had he felt a mighty presence around him.

"I do."

James nodded. "Good. I do too. I'm not scared, not now I know Adaline and Courtney have you. Before you showed up, I was terrified of dying and leaving them alone. Now I'm tired of hanging on."

Heat stung the back of Jake's eyes.

His father's eyes clouded, and then Jake realized his own had filled with tears as well.

"I'm grateful you came. That you gave us a chance to meet. I love you, son."

James reached out, but Jake didn't take his hand. Instead, he stood and paced to the window. The dusty ground outside, covered in fallen leaves, looked stark and bleak, and the overcast sky made the room feel dark.

"I own everything in the house, so it's all yours and the girls'. I don't know how much you'll want to cart back to Logan Meadows. That's up to you. If you don't want anything, that's fine too. Remember the banker, Hugh Hexum. If you need anything, you can go to him. Told me when the time came, he'd help all he could."

Jake kept his gaze trained outside. His father wanted forgiveness. Jake struggled to swallow back the lump of grief he felt growing inside. Would saying the words really mean anything at all after all these years? Anger had poisoned his heart over the abandonment. What was forgiveness anyway, but a silly way to relieve guilt? Doing and being meant more than anything else.

Outside, a chipmunk raced under a handful of leaves and, after a moment, poked his head out the other side.

Jake sighed. Heat radiated in his chest. He might have only known his pa a few days, but maybe that was enough. Enough time to change the past. Should he try? Could he? Three small words . . . *I forgive you.*

He squared his shoulders and turned, realizing the deed was right.

Stared.

There was no mistaking.

His father had passed quietly over into eternity.

Chapter Fourteen

A profound sorrow gripped Jake as he stood in the church graveyard, staring down into the open hole nestling his father's coffin. Bunches of tall feather grass, swayed by the crisp autumn breeze, lined the small fence surrounding three quarters of the grounds. Two men he didn't know stood on either side of the grave, shoveling in heaping mounds of light, sandy soil while a handful of other mourners meandered away, back toward town after paying their final respects to a longtime friend. Two days had passed since his father had died, feeling much like a dream.

Courtney and Mrs. Torry returned ten minutes too late. Once they were home, Jake had set out and found Adaline helping in the restaurant. As soon as she took one look at his face, she knew what he'd come to say and ran the whole way home. Since then, the hours had swept by in a blur. Not much had been decided with all the crying, but he didn't begrudge his sisters that. He'd be a liar if he claimed not to have shed a few tears himself.

The preacher waited a few feet away, giving Jake and his sisters, as well as Mrs. Torry, time and space to grieve.

Jake had traveled to Newport to discover his name, not to feel this canyon-sized regret that threatened to pull him inside the gaping crevasse at his feet.

Adaline stood on his right, trying to keep warm in her black dress and shawl. Her eyes, a hurtful red from all the tears she'd shed since Tuesday, held a mountain of pain. Jake was thankful her employer, Mrs. Bennett, had insisted she take a few weeks off tutoring. That, at least, would give Adaline some time to grieve.

Mrs. Torry, with her ever-stoic expression, stood with an arm firmly around Adaline's back, as if holding his sister steady. Every now and then, the woman pressed a white linen handkerchief to the corner of her eye.

Courtney and Wil Lemon stood on the opposite side of the grave, the man's uninterested expression in opposition with the arm possessively draped over his youngest sister's shoulders. When the time arrived to leave town, there'd be a fight. Jake had no illusions about that.

He was good with his gun, but he wasn't a hardened killer—not like the man standing only a few feet away. Jake didn't have a score of notches on the inside of his gun belt either. Today, out of respect for his father, he'd left his weapon in his room. Not so Wil Lemon.

Jake rubbed the back of his neck and stretched his aching back muscles. How he missed Daisy. Besides the cattle drives, this was the longest they'd ever been apart. A gust of wind scattered some leaves at his feet, sending a chill into his heart. *What will Daisy do if I'm killed here in Newport?* He thought of Chase and Jessie, Gabe and Mrs. Hollyhock. And for the first time ever, he thought of his mother, hoping she'd still be in Logan Meadows when he returned—if he returned.

"I had my reasons, Jake, ones I'll not share with you. You can hate me if you want. I'm sure you already do."

He remembered the day in the laundry house when he'd thought her unfeeling. Now, he understood. She'd begged James to reconsider his decision for her son's sake, more than her own.

But nothing would change his father's mind. She'd become bitter and hateful, turning to the bottle to relieve her pain. His face, so much like his father's, was a constant reminder of the man who had used and abandoned her.

Finished, the gravediggers backed away, the whole scene passing in utter silence except for the faraway sounds of the town, and the rustling of the parched leaves yet to dry completely and disappear into the earth.

When someone tapped his shoulder, Jake turned.

The preacher. Jake couldn't remember his name.

"May I speak with you privately?" the preacher whispered and gestured a few feet away.

Jake nodded and followed. His gaze moved with Wil and Courtney as they turned and made their way back to the horse and buggy sitting on the road next to the cemetery's white picket fence.

The preacher, a tall, thick fellow with a full head of curly dark hair, gave him an appreciative smile. His wide-set eyes looked deeply into Jake's. "Will you be leaving soon?"

"As soon as things are squared away and a few things packed. The girls have some belongings they'd like to take. Can't blame 'em, I guess."

What about Dalton, his conscience whispered.

"You don't want anything?"

Jake shook his head.

The preacher took a deep breath of the crisp air. "I'm relieved you showed up when you did. Leaving the girls alone weighed heavily on James's mind. He told me about you a few years ago. He longed to see you, some way, somehow. I'm pleased the two of you finally met. To say your good-byes."

Jake suspected he would feel better if he'd forgiven his father when the man had asked. Shifting from foot to foot, he glanced away. Adaline and Mrs. Torry stood at the grave; Courtney was inside the buggy, sitting next to the gunslinger.

"I'm glad too. Learnin' I had a father was a surprise I wasn't expecting."

The preacher inched closer and lowered his voice. "I hope you don't think me forward, but I have to say I'm worried about Courtney. She's not doing herself any favors stepping out with Wil Lemon. I believe in conversion as much as the next preacher, but I don't hold much hope for that young man. There's a black cloud that follows him around. Bad things happen. I doubt he'll live to a ripe old age, if you catch my meaning."

"Can't someone send for a marshal?"

"No one's ever been able to make any charges stick. He's slippery; accusations run off him like water off a gull's back. His friends back up every word he says. Give him alibis every time he kills, saying he was provoked and the shooting was self-defense."

Pausing for a moment, the preacher added, "There was an issue last year with a young woman from the neighboring town who fell off a cliff. Her parents insist he killed her, but they have no proof. The last sheriff, before he was gunned down by an unknown, was aware. Was trying to catch him up, but he could do only so much without evidence. And now he's been killed. I'll rest easier when you take Courtney out of Newport."

Jake waited to respond because Adaline was on her way over to where he and the preacher stood. Mrs. Torry remained at the grave.

"Mrs. Torry and I are walking home," Adaline said in a small voice. "She wants to stop by the mercantile so she can pick up some sugar to bake a cake."

"The women from the church will be dropping by some baked things, Adaline," the preacher said. His eyes held a deep, abiding sorrow.

She shrugged. "I know, but it's what Mrs. Torry does when she's upset. She says it's for us, but keeping her hands busy will be good for her heart."

Jake plainly saw his father had gained many people's respect and love. "All right," he said. "I'm about ready to head back with Courtney. If it starts to rain, stay in the store, and I'll come get you with the buggy."

She smiled and laid a small hand on the sleeve of his coat. "Thank you, Jake."

He watched as she hurried away. She reached the grave, and Mrs. Torry joined her. The two headed down the path.

"I best be going too, Preacher," he said, wishing he could remember the man's name. "Thank you for your sermon."

"You're welcome." Concern crossed the man's eyes. "If you send word the day before you pull out, I may be able to help." His gaze strayed to the buggy. "With Wil."

Surprised, Jake couldn't hide his astonishment. "Help?"

"I don't want to see anyone get hurt. And I surely don't want to see Courtney remain here with the likes of him. Perhaps with both of us attending to detail, we'll make your departure uneventful and safe."

Jake felt the first smile he'd had in days. He thrust out his hand. "I'll do that, Preacher. Thank you."

The preacher gave him an amused grin. "It's Randall Hensley."

Jake nodded. "Thank you, again." Feeling optimistic, he turned and headed for the buggy.

Chapter Fifteen

Dalton cursed under his breath when the light sprinkles that had begun an hour ago turned into a downpour. He loathed going back into the dark confines of the train car. His head was clearer today than since this nightmare begun. Yesterday he'd started hiding the food the guards offered. He wandered to the far side of their boundary and buried the meals the best he could, or took it into the outhouse.

His stomach burned with hunger. His head ached from the lack of sustenance, and he felt a little weak. Still, he was sure he could take the guards, one at a time, if given the chance. At the moment, only one sat under the rooftop shanty on the side of the enclosure closest to the road. The man's head rested on the palm of his hand as he dozed away the afternoon.

Merryweather had not been as disciplined with the food. With Dalton's clearer head, he could easily spot the man's drugged state when he ingested a new dose of whatever the guards were giving them.

Standing in the rain at the perimeter of the fence, he wondered what the young woman's mention of Logan Meadows had meant. That couldn't have been a coincidence. The location had to imply something, and yet nothing had happened. He was sure he'd never seen or met her before, so how did she know him?

The puzzle was ever-darkening—except he knew Alaska was waiting on his arrival. Whoever owned the mine had a good ruse going. He could work the men as hard as he liked, and no one would be the wiser. When they died, they'd be replaced with new slaves. No one dared venture over to the holding pen of hardened killers and equally dangerous guards. These townsfolk were good and buffaloed.

In his weakened condition, discouragement descended. He thought of Susanna, back in Logan Meadows, and the plan he'd been making to return to the homey little settlement in Wyoming, even though he'd lost her to Albert. The sheriff was one lucky man, winning Susanna's heart. Dalton had once thought that might be him, but their match hadn't transpired. Still, he'd made a lot of good friends in the town. Now, unless he corralled some energy and found a way to escape, they'd never know what happened to him.

He let his mind wander to the young woman who seemed to be sending him a secret communication. Who was she? Had her words been some sort of clandestine message she'd been sent here to deliver? She was brave and a bit defiant. He'd been moved by the intensity of her dark blue eyes, even from ten feet away. Would she come back? He prayed to God she would. He didn't have much time to spare.

A rider approached in the rain. He was a large man, one Dalton hadn't seen out here before. Seeing the stranger rein up, Dalton stepped away from the fence, babbled something about cherry pie, and leaned precariously to one side as he lifted his face to the sky. He didn't want to tip off his captors he was on to their scam.

"Rigley," the large man shouted, making the sleeping guard jump to his feet. "Where's Durst?" His head jerked around as he looked for the missing guard.

Dalton dropped his chin to gaze at the mud around his boots when the newcomer looked his way. He picked up one foot to a loud sucking sound, and gave the angry-faced man a sleepy-eyed gaze.

"He was here a minute ago, Strangely," the guard whined. "How do I know? Guess he snuck off. It's cold and wet out here."

"Shut up. Neither of you has a brain between you."

"Don't say that."

The tall man cut a look at Dalton. "Either of the men giving you any problems?"

"Naw, they's as gentle as lambs. Long as we keep 'em fed, it's like they ain't even here. Not like the last noisy batch."

"Shut up! How many times do I have to tell you that? When Durst returns, have him come see me at the sheriff's office. I don't know what's taking the ship so long, but if we don't get these two up to Alaska while the weather is agreeable, we may be stuck with 'em. That's a problem I don't want hanging around my neck."

"I could sell 'em someplace else, Strangely. No need to do everything *he* says. We could cut out their tongues so they can't tell no one they've been shanghaied."

The man named Strangely glared. "Your mouth is unbelievable. How many times do I have to shut you up?"

Just as Dalton had suspected. Once they were aboard a ship north bound, their chances of escape would be practically nil.

The approaching mud-sucking sound made Dalton look over his shoulder. Jay Merryweather had come out of the train car and was on his way to Dalton's side. His lips wobbled and he wiped a hand over his face, now drenched in rain.

The small fellow was so thin, he most likely wouldn't survive an ocean voyage. If Dalton could get away, he'd have to try to take Merryweather with him.

Will I be strong enough when the time comes? Each passing day, Dalton's strength ebbed with the tiny amount of food he ate. He'd have to make a move soon.

Chapter Sixteen

Still wearing her black dress, Adaline circled the table with the coffeepot, refilling Jake's cup and then poor, tired Mrs. Torry's. Dark circles had deepened under the woman's eyes in the last few days. She stared into the brown liquid, lost in thought.

Adaline supposed they were all trying to figure out what would happen now that the horrible event had finally come to pass. She glanced at Courtney and lifted the pot in question.

Courtney shook her head. She had changed out of her mourning dress and slipped on something more comfortable after the last of the guests left. Several hot dishes, two half-eaten pies, a platter of cookies, and one white cake crowded the middle of the table, waiting to be put away, as well as an almost-empty bottle of red wine. Although the majority of Oregon forbade alcohol, Newport had the distinction of being the only "wet" city.

"What now?" Courtney asked, her voice sounding much like the little girl Adaline remembered.

Everyone looked to Jake.

Adaline set the hot coffeepot on a trivet and lowered herself into her chair. "We don't have to make any major decisions quite yet. We'll be all right for some time to come."

Jake's brow crinkled and he didn't look up.

Was he trying to decide when to go home to Logan Meadows? She didn't like the thought of him leaving.

He lifted his coffee cup and took a sip, his gaze staying far away from hers.

"What are your plans, Jake?" Courtney asked. Her sister wiped the bottom of her fork across her plate, getting the last of the pie crumbs, but she stopped with the fork midair. "Will you be going home soon?"

"No choices have to be made tonight," Mrs. Torry said softly. "Give yourselves some time to come to grips. I'm sure Jake isn't ready to leave."

The ticking of the clock in the next room seemed amplified. Adaline imagined the pendulum moving to the beats of her heart and thought of her meeting with Mr. Hexum. He'd been agreeable, but she'd seen him in action before. How long before he came calling for real?

"Exactly, Mrs. Torry. For Jake, he's just found his father, only to lose him so quickly." Her gaze connected with his for only a few seconds, but long enough to feel like something was off. What was troubling him? "Jake, is there something on your mind?"

Then she remembered going to the prison camp. *The captive! With Papa dying, I totally forgot about him. But Jake hasn't.*

Jake gave a small shrug. His eyes tracked over to Courtney, and then back to her. "There is something I want to speak with you about."

"Would you like me to leave?" Mrs. Torry asked.

Courtney gasped. "You're family, Mrs. Torry." Her eyes teared up.

Adaline had never seen Courtney so brittle.

"Courtney's right," Jake said. "Nothing I'm gonna say can't be said in front of you."

The housekeeper reached over and took one of Courtney's hands.

"Right before your pa passed away, he asked a favor."

Everyone sat forward.

This was something he hadn't shared before. Adaline wondered what was so important.

"He requested I take you both back to Logan Meadows when I leave. So we can be a family. It's a good idea. I told him I would."

Courtney bolted to her feet, Mrs. Torry's hand falling away. "I won't go. You can't make me. You're not my father any more than Adaline is my mother."

Adaline's happiness at Jake's words was tempered by her sister's actions. "Don't you care that I'd miss you?" she asked, setting her cup back on its saucer. "Logan Meadows sounds nice, as do Daisy and the Logans. And the rest of Jake's friends. I can't wait to go and meet them all."

Courtney wrapped her arms around her middle. "That's because you don't have a sweetheart here, Adaline. And you've always said you'd like to move away. I plan to stay in Newport for the rest of my life. Then I'll be close to both Mama and Papa forever."

It's sweetheart now, is it? Adaline used her napkin, thinking how best to address the situation. She loathed Wil and the mesmerizing hold he had over her baby sister.

"At least you're finally being honest calling him your sweetheart." Setting aside her own growing irritation, she stood and hurried to Courtney's chair. She tried to put an arm across her shoulder, but Courtney pulled away.

"I'm old enough to make my own decisions," Courtney said sternly, looking between her and Jake. "I'm not leaving

Newport." Her hands fisted. "You have nothing to worry about, Jake. You can stop your scowling right this minute."

"*I'm* not old enough to legally make my own decisions, Courtney. And you're certainly not!" Adaline threw back, perplexed at her sister's strong reaction. Starting over fresh sounded good. *Exciting.* Their lives would be a clean slate. "You'd rather stay here so Wil Lemon can break your heart and ruin your life instead of taking Jake up on his offer?"

Jake was now on his feet, as well as Mrs. Torry.

Courtney glared at them all. "So what if I like Wil? No, I *love* Wil. He'd never do anything to hurt me."

"You're too young to know what love is," Adaline shot back. She couldn't go and leave her little sister behind. Courtney needed someone to look out for her. "You're fifteen. He's your first beau. And much too old."

"And you're jealous," Courtney spat back.

Jake came around the table and stood between the two. "Regardless of who is or isn't old enough, as I said before, I think the move is a good idea. And it's what your pa wanted." He pulled out the note James had given him the day he died. "Your father wrote out his wishes, in case you didn't believe me. You'll like Logan Meadows. The people are good. Myself, I'm anxious to get back."

"Then go," Courtney screeched. "Just don't think you're dragging me along, whether Papa wanted it or not. Where would we live? I'm sure Jake doesn't even know," she said in a more complacent tone.

"I'm workin' on that," Jake said, his voice low. "I didn't even know you two existed until I arrived. Give me a chance. I'll work things out."

"I won't live in a bunkhouse."

Color came up in Jake's face and his lips pulled down. "I never said you would. Told you Daisy and I have a small place we're plannin' on livin' in, but there isn't room for the two of you. I'll get you settled. Somewhere you can make friends. There are several young ladies I know you'd like."

"Stop speaking as if I'm going, Jake. You can wish all you want, but I'm staying here and marrying Wil. It won't be long before I'm Mrs. Wil Lemon."

What an awful thought. Adaline resisted rolling her eyes. "You want to be Mrs. Lemon, and be known as a sourpuss?"

"Hush," Jake bit out with an angry look. "That's not helping."

"Be reasonable, Courtney," she tried more softly. "Wil's a ranch hand, just like Jake, but doesn't own any land or a house like our brother does. Where will you live? How will his salary pay for a wife and baby someday?"

"He's looking into a rental on Bee Street. Said he'll put a payment down just as soon as I pick which one I like the best."

Shaking her head, Adaline scoffed. "When pigs fly."

Jake sent her a look that said to keep her cool, then glanced away.

Courtney glared at her older sister. "Besides, we'll have some money when we sell the house. You're just jealous because I'm younger than you. You wish you had a fiancé like I do. I love Wil. He's a good man."

Adaline thought the opposite. After the scoundrel had his way with Courtney, he'd toss her sister into the gutter and move on to the next foolish young woman.

Looking more than a bit miserable, Jake cleared his throat. "That's the other bit of information your father left to me to tell," he said. "I'm sorry to be the bearer of bad news, but he lost the house last year."

A jolt of dread hit Adaline. "What? Lost it to whom? What do you mean? Papa wouldn't keep such an important secret to himself."

"He didn't want to distress you. Everything inside is yours." He looked between her and Courtney.

"Who's the new owner?" Adaline asked, feeling her stomach clench. Seemed she knew the answer before Jake could utter a word.

"The banker. Hugh Hexum. Your father said he's an upright fellow. Said he would let us stay as long as we needed. But for me, that won't be long at all. I want to be on an eastbound train by early next week."

Adaline's heart fell. Jake might want to be on the train next week, but she knew Hexum would do everything in his power to keep her from ever leaving town.

Chapter Seventeen

At Jake's pronouncement, Adaline's face went white and Courtney dashed out of the room to her bedroom, slamming the door. Seemed his youngest sister was set on ruining her life. Now that all the bombshells were out, he needed to figure out what he would do about Dalton.

"Jake, may I speak with you in private?" Adaline had circled the table and now stood next to him, worry etched on her face.

Mrs. Torry reached for the leftovers and started for the kitchen, leaving him and Adaline alone.

"Sure." He escorted her into the parlor and they went to stand by the front window. The rain that had begun to fall two hours ago had stopped, and now only puddles remained on the walk.

She fiddled with the black cuff at the end of her sleeve. Jake couldn't imagine what was making her so nervous.

"I have a confession to make. When I was at work on Tuesday, before I'd learned Papa had passed, I was thinking about you. You and this unwise idea about the prisoner waiting on the ship." She briefly looked into his face. "I wanted to prove you wrong so you'd give up the far-fetched notion about rescuing him."

Jake snagged her gaze, hoping she hadn't gone and done something stupid.

"I had the opportunity to take the noontime meal to the prisoners."

"What?" he barked. He hadn't meant to draw her into his trouble, and yet he'd done just that.

"Please, Jake, let me finish. When I arrived, I was scrambling for a way to find out. I didn't have much time and the guards were hurrying me away. Finally, I blurted out some gibberish that didn't really even make sense, but added Logan Meadows to the statement all the while watching the prisoners for a reaction. I hate to say this, but I'm sure your assumption is correct. The tallest of the two definitely heard what I said and seemed surprised."

Fear hit Jake right between his eyes. *Adaline down at the prison camp—alone!* The memory of what he used to feel each night Daisy went to work in the Bright Nugget swamped him. The danger she'd faced working there hadn't just been about the men and the way she earned her money, but the risk of a flying bullet, a drunken brawl, or a flashing knife blade.

"I can't believe my ears. What possessed you to do a stupid thing like that? Without asking me first?"

She jerked her shoulders straight. "Jake, calm down. Nothing happened."

"This time."

Her brow arched. "Like I said, I wanted to prove you wrong so you'd give up. I intended to tell you right away, but then Papa died and I forgot. I'm sorry—not about what I did, but for forgetting to tell you."

He could understand that. The whole house had been under a shroud of sorrow since Tuesday. "I'm angry with you, Adaline.

You had no right to butt in like that. You could have been hurt."
Or worse. I don't like to consider that.

She waved a hand. "Those men watching over the compound are thick. They report to Lee Strangely—but they don't even seem like real soldiers. If you say your friend couldn't be guilty of a crime, especially since it's been such a short time since the letter he sent to Logan Meadows, perhaps some sort of criminal activity is going on. Do you know what I'm getting at?"

Jake ignored her questions. He wasn't letting her get any more involved than she already was. "What did this man look like up close? We'll call him Dalton, because that's who I believe he is."

"Well . . ." Her face colored up and she glanced away.

Jake frowned. *What's this about?*

"He's very tall. Has wide shoulders and his eyes are light brown, like the caramel apples we make at Halloween, really unusual."

"You were close enough to see his eyes?"

"Well, yes." A small smile played around her lips. "The way he was staring made me a bit jumpy, and yet I couldn't pull away my own gaze. His features were sharp. What I could see of his hair under the prison clothing cap was thick and dark."

Her voice had gone soft, and Jake wondered what she was thinking—or better yet, feeling.

"Then, that fixed it. He's Dalton. I've been on the end of his scrutiny before myself. Those first few hours after the Union Pacific accident were tense. He was responsible for a train car full of money, and he wasn't taking his job lightly." Jake mulled over what had to be done. "With no one else to right things, I'll have to do it. Without law, man falls into depravity. I'd be as bad as his captors if I turned a blind eye to his plight."

Adaline turned to him, her hands clasped in front of her skirt. This was the first time in two days he'd seen some light in her eyes. Keeping her out of this would be trouble.

He warned, "You are not helping me do this."

"You *need* my help. You can't do it alone. I know everyone and places you have no idea about. What's your plan?"

She was right, of course. He didn't want to endanger her, but Dalton needed someone on the outside. Adaline knew a lot more about Newport than he did.

"I haven't made up my mind yet."

"Jake, I promise I'll be careful." Her voice sounded blunt with a hint of annoyance. "We don't have a moment to spare. The ship may be docking right now. We need to make a plan; if we don't, it'll be too late for your friend."

She was right. He'd waited as long as he should.

"What about Courtney? She's going to be a problem when the time comes to leave. Getting her on the train against her will, and without alerting Lemon, will be tough enough. Now we've also got to get Dalton aboard without tipping off the authorities."

"Newport has no authorities."

"I know that," he replied. "That's part of the problem."

What he wouldn't give to have Albert here, Logan Meadow's trusted sheriff. As fate planned, this responsibility fell to Jake's shoulders alone.

From what he'd seen, Adaline was right about the guards and the setup. Something fishy was going on. Recently, he'd read a short article in the newspaper about how unsuspecting men were being shanghaied to work on ships, bound for just about anywhere. Many of the abductions were taking place in San Francisco, the exact city where Dalton was living.

The time to act was now. As Adaline had said, the ship bound for Alaska might be docking this very minute. He'd pay Lee Strangely a visit first thing tomorrow morning.

Chapter Eighteen

Jake watched as Lee Strangely looked up from his seat at the sheriff's desk. The man had a knife in his hands and was whittling something. His bald head reminded Jake of an ostrich egg Sarah had showed him once in a book. A pink scar came over the top of his head and slashed across his forehead. Even though he was sitting, Jake could tell the man must weigh over two hundred pounds. Not someone he intended to tangle with now, or ever.

The man's eyes narrowed the moment he realized someone he didn't know had dared to step through his door. "Do I know you?" Strangely asked, his gravelly voice impatient.

Jake purposely wrung his hands. He swallowed, making a show of unease. "N-no, sir. You don't. I'm new to town. Just came in a few days ago."

"What do you want?" Strangely bit out. He stood and came out from behind the desk, a six-shooter strapped to his leg and covered with a flap like a regimental army holster.

"Name's Jake Garrison," he replied, using Gabe's last name in case Strangely was acquainted with his father.

How ironic. He finally had a last name, but couldn't use it. Sadness over his father filled him, but he couldn't afford to be distracted unless he wanted to end up dead.

"I hail from Minnesota, here to hunt ancient relics, bones, fossils, anything. Just wanted to check in and let the sheriff know I'll be exploring down by the train depot."

"You can't do that."

Hiking an eyebrow, Jake tipped his head. "You're the sheriff?"

"No."

Jake let a smile grow across his face. "That's a relief. When do you expect him back? He's the only one who can grant or deny permission about diggin' in a town." *I hope this fellow doesn't know anything about the law since I'm making things up as I go.*

"There isn't a sheriff in this town. I'm with the Army, so what I say goes."

Strangely squared his shoulders and gazed at Jake, not the least bit intimidated. Just like the guards watching over Dalton, Strangely's uniform had seen better days. He didn't act or speak like any officer Jake had ever met, and didn't display any rank on his shoulders.

"Sorry," Jake said. "In most things that's true, but not when the issue involves federal doings in search of material for museums."

If Strangely decided to question him, then Jake would have to think fast. Sarah was better equipped for a conversation like this. A sheen of sweat broke out on his forehead as he spoke again.

"Give me your superior officer's name, and I'll have the director of bone-finding contact him. Might take a day or two, though. I'll be puttering around, starting later today. I only came in now because I was already given the third degree by one of your guards. If he interferes again, I'll have to call in a federal marshal for backup. I'm only here for a short period and need to make the time count." He shifted his weight, certain that Strangely's operation didn't want any lawmen poking around. "I won't hurt nothing. Just dig a few holes, collect a few bones or shells. You won't even know I'm around."

Two bright red blotches stained Strangely's cheeks. The spots appeared about the time Jake asked for his commanding officer's name. Pushing this fellow's temper was actually a bit amusing. He reminded Jake of Dwight Hoskins back in Logan Meadows.

"Who told you to talk to me?" Strangely asked.

That's a strange question. "What?"

"Who sent you here?"

"Oh . . ." Risky to tell a falsehood in case Strangely were to ask the guard, but he'd have to take that chance. "Your guard. I asked who was in charge. Now, the name please of your commanding officer so I won't run into any problems in the coming days. I'd like to get this straightened out. I'm on a schedule I aim to keep."

Strangely's lip curled in disgust. As he opened his mouth to reply, perhaps to answer Jake's question, someone opened the door and entered.

For some reason, Jake only dared a quick glance.

"What's going on?" a man dressed in business attire asked Strangely.

"Nothin', Hexum," Strangely bit out. Turning his gaze to Jake, he jerked his head toward the door, indicating Jake should leave.

Shocked, Jake kept his attention trained away from Hexum, in case they had dealings later on regarding the rented house. Bad timing, to be sure.

"Go on, get. You can do your diggin'; just stay out of trouble."

So, the banker who Costner thought the world of knew Strangely well enough to stop in for a chat. Was he some part of this sham? He looks like a respectable fellow, but appearances don't mean squat.

Jake filed away those thoughts and stepped out. He paused just out of sight with an ear turned to the door he'd left ajar an inch, hoping neither man noticed.

He'd need to purchase some things at the mercantile to make his disguise more convincing. A hand trowel, some sort of pack to sling over his shoulder. Maybe he'd even get a monocle to stick in his eye to better look the part when he went to work, scratching about the dirt like some chicken.

He chuckled inwardly. Surely, Dalton would happily pay him back the expenses he incurred to spring the man. He'd be darned thankful not to be sailing to Alaska.

About to step away, Jake heard Hexum's commanding voice from inside.

"Malinda Plummer, wife of our lighthouse keeper, just came down from Yaquina Head. After making a deposit, she informed me the *Tigress* has been spotted on the horizon. Should be making port by tonight or tomorrow morning. You make sure the two prisoners are ready to be moved. Give 'em twice the normal dose. We can't risk any more problems, not like we had last month with the civilian. Some around town have become suspicious. Any more shoddy work and the guards will find themselves on the *Tigress*, headed to my mine, and not as guards. As well as the dolts in San Francisco, since they're sending us fewer and fewer men. Is that understood?"

Not wanting to get caught, Jake quickly stepped away before either noticed the partially opened door. He'd heard enough.

After he freed Dalton and the other man, he'd alert Albert. Surely men now in Alaska had been reported missing by their families.

Until then, if Jake ever wanted to be a bridegroom, he'd have to be very careful. Otherwise, he'd end up on the *Tigress*, right next to Dalton and his friend headed to a life of slavery.

Chapter Nineteen

Adaline took her father's pipe from the drawer beside the bed and set it gently in a stack of keepsakes she'd take to Logan Meadows. The scent of tobacco lingered, even though he hadn't smoked for more than six months. She remembered sitting in his lap as a little girl, looking at the black print on white paper as he read the newspaper after a long day. She blinked away a stab of pain. He was gone.

Courtney glanced her way. "I love the smell of his pipe."

Her throat feeling tight, she nodded. "I know. I do too."

She and Courtney had been packing all day. Knowing everything couldn't come along, Adaline had obtained several large crates from Mrs. Bennett, who'd also lent her Freddy to help for the day after school, since they'd suspended his tutoring sessions. Adaline thought the gesture exceedingly generous of her former boss. Adaline had given notice, telling her employer she'd need to leave with Jake whenever they were ready to travel. She wasn't certain of the date.

"What should I do with Papa's clothes?" Courtney asked, gazing in her father's wardrobe with a woeful expression pulling her face. Her nose, a strawberry red from all her tears, accented her wobbly voice.

Her little sister was not taking the last few days well. Thankfully, Wil Lemon had stayed away since the funeral, giving Adaline time to convince her sister that going to Logan Meadows was the best thing for both of them. A new town. A fresh start. As well as a brother they'd both just met.

Their father had wanted them to be a family, so Adaline couldn't go without Courtney. Still, as much as Adaline persuaded, she was uncertain of her sister's feelings. When the time came to step onto the train, she didn't know what Courtney would do. Going meant leaving Wil Lemon behind.

"Fold them nicely and put them into the trunk for the poor. Someone will be happy to get them, I'm sure."

A loud crash resonated up the stairs. Freddy was helping Mrs. Torry sort out the kitchen. The boy hadn't been overly excited when he'd been told what his job would be, but he'd dug in when asked. Perhaps some of the lessons she'd given him on duty had sunken in.

Courtney's head whipped toward the door. "Oh! I wonder what precious keepsake is now in a hundred pieces? I hate to think of all the things we're leaving behind."

Adaline put an arm around her shoulder. "Mrs. Torry was nice to offer to let us store a few boxes at her house. With the cost of shipping, we can't take much now, but perhaps when we find work in Logan Meadows, that will be different. This gives us a little time. As well as Mrs. Bennett offering to sell what she could in the mercantile, for a percentage of the profit. The rest we'll give away. You'll see. Once the belongings are gone, you won't miss them." She put on a brave face for her sister. "And I'll be happy to think of our things in the hands of the needy."

"And all of Papa's books? I can't bear to just leave them here for whoever moves in, like Mrs. Bennett suggested. The new inhabitants might throw them out or use them to start their fire, or for toilet paper, as the hill people do." At the ghastly thought, Courtney clutched the shirt she'd been folding and clamped the garment to her chest. "Papa loved them so. He'd be horrified."

"That's why we're not doing that. Since they're unbreakable, we'll crate them and send them cheaply overland with a mule freighter. Jake's offer to pay was very generous. He thinks the new bookstore owner in Logan Meadows will be interested in them. At least then, we can make *some* money toward our new life. Papa won't mind if they go to good homes. Whoever pays for them will love them as he did. That's a consolation, at least."

Courtney picked at a thread on her sleeve. "*If* the shop owner wants such a large lot of books all at once," she said hesitantly.

"We'll have to hope she does."

Downstairs, the front door opened and then closed.

Jake must be home. "You keep working, and I'll be right back. I have something I want to discuss with Jake," Adaline said, heading for the bedroom door.

Jake had slipped away after breakfast without saying a word. She was sure the reason must have something to do with freeing his friend Dalton Babcock.

Hurrying down the stairway, she arrived at her room just as he was about to shut the door. "Jake."

The door that was almost closed opened slowly. Several items she'd never seen before were laid out on the bed.

"What're you doing? How could you leave this morning without a word to me?"

"You had packing to do. I'd rather you do that than get involved with my plan."

She crossed her arms. He wasn't going to just brush her off. "What's your plan?"

"Spring Dalton Babcock and the other fellow and put them on an outbound train before anyone is the wiser. I don't need your help. I can handle this on my own."

Keeping her temper in check, Adaline moved into the room and quietly clicked the door closed. When she turned to address him face-to-face, she was taken aback. "What is it? You look strange."

He cut his gaze away, letting a deep sigh escape his lips. He glanced at the items on the bed and then back at her. "The ship from Alaska was spotted. Should be docking by tonight or tomorrow."

"Oh, no." She stepped forward and grasped his arm. "We must act quickly. The *Tigress* usually only stays in port for a handful of days."

"What I'm planning is dangerous. I'm worried you'll slow me down and possibly mess up my only chance. Once the guards are on to me, that's it."

She let Jake's hurtful words fall away. He was anxious. Nervous for his friend. She wouldn't hold them against him. Besides, he'd only known her such a short amount of time. He had no idea how clever she could be.

"Jake, think of Daisy. What will happen to her if you don't return? Contemplate that for a few minutes before you discount my help. I've lived here all my life. I know hiding places. I know the train schedules. I can get my hands on things you might need without arousing suspicion. Like it or not, you *need* me."

His brow tented over one eye. "I can see you've given this a lot of thought."

"You bet I have. I'm your sister, aren't I? I think just like you." She could tell he was weighing what she'd said carefully. She smiled, looking him in the eyes. "Jake?"

"You're right about everything you just said. Before we make any plans, I need to know if you have a trusted friend, someone I could go to for help in case something goes wrong. I feel like a fish out of water here. I wish I was back in Wyoming. I'd know what to do then."

The seriousness of his expression made her swallow.

"A person who holds some respectability in the town," he added.

She thought for a minute. "Yes. Malinda Plummer. She's the wife of the lighthouse keeper. They've been living at the lighthouse for five years. We're good friends. Both Malinda *and* Frank can be trusted. I'd go to them with any problem."

He nodded. "Fine. We don't want to involve them unless things go wrong. The fewer people who know what we're plannin', the better. What time does the morning eastbound train depart?"

"Seven."

"Fine. This is what we'll do. I'll take my excavating tools late in the afternoon and—"

"Excavating tools? I don't understand."

"That's my cover. I'm posing as if I've been sent here from a Minnesota museum."

"What do you know about museums?"

"Not much. Just something that popped into my head when I needed it. Good thing those guards know even less than I do. Won't be hard to fool 'em. I'll get the lay of the land the best I can. If the opportunity presents itself, I'll even try and get close enough to perhaps say something to Dalton. Alert him in some way, so he can help when the time comes." He withdrew money from his pocket and peeled off two ten-dollar bills. "Can you go to the depot and buy three tickets to Logan Meadows?"

"Of course, as soon as we're finished talking. But three?"

"It might look suspicious only buying two. Buy three, so the depot master will think they're for me, you, and Courtney. When it's time for us to really depart, I'll purchase more, saying I lost the other two."

She cocked her head, still not quite understanding.

"We're taking the other fella as well."

"Jake!"

"I know, I know, but from what I learned today, I'm certain all the men who have passed through the camp onto the *Tigress* and shipped away to Alaska have been hit over the head and shanghaied. They're slaving in Hexum's gold mine."

She gasped and took a step back. "Hexum?"

Jake nodded. "He came into the sheriff's office when I was there, not knowing who I was. I eavesdropped after I stepped outside. He's calling the shots."

Bile rose in her throat. "I should've known."

"What do you mean?"

"Papa might have thought highly of the bank owner, but that was only because he didn't know the man has been pressuring me into marrying him for the past year. He offered to forgive all of my father's loans if I'd comply. I saw him the other day before Papa's passing. He said something that piqued my curiosity. Something about me changing my tune soon enough. Now I understand. I thought I had the house to fall back on. The sale of such a property would keep Courtney and me for a long time. Now, without it, he thinks I'll fall into his arms." She shivered at the thought.

For the first time ever, Jake drew her into his arms. "That'll never happen. You'll always have a home with me and Daisy. I can promise you that."

"What if Daisy doesn't want me and Courtney? That's a houseful. Especially to a newlywed."

"Believe me, she will. Daisy's the sweetest woman I know."

Adaline rolled her eyes. "That's because she's in love with you, Jake. She's not in love with your sisters."

"You'll see," he began, but frowned when a small sound came from the other side of the door.

Courtney?

Without hesitation, Jake jerked the door wide and Freddy fell into the room. He had blueberry jam spread across his mouth as he smiled up at Adaline.

"So, yer gonna break them prisoners out of jail?" The boy's eyes shone brightly. "I want to help."

"Freddy! It's not polite to eavesdrop," Adaline spat out angrily, trying to figure the best way to handle this new fly in the ointment. "You should be ashamed of yourself. We were doing no such planning." She gave him a direct stare.

"I heard ya."

Chicken feathers. There's no changing his mind. I'll just have to make it clear all he has to lose.

"Remember when I caught you eating the chocolate bars from the store, Freddy, and you assured me you were just helping your parents with the inventory? How I thought one thing, but you enlightened me with the truth," she said sternly, folding her arms across her chest and narrowing her eyes. "Or the many, many times you showed up for tutoring at the very last minute, but you told me you'd lost your new shoes, or your hat, or your schoolbooks? How you cried, saying you didn't want to get into trouble and to please keep quiet? What about the time you forgot to lock the mercantile door and all those expensive items were stolen? I took the blame to save your hide, didn't I?"

He nodded, his eyes wide.

"I have several more examples, if you'd like me to go on. With each, I protected you. Kept the truth to myself. I could tell your parents everything, if you'd think they'd like to know."

His head quickly jiggled back and forth. She took her hankie from her skirt pocket and handed it to the boy, gesturing to his mouth, and he began wiping away the jam.

"Will you keep my private conversation with Jake to yourself since pressing your ear to the door is very shameful? If you don't, I'll tell your parents of your tomfooleries, and not bat an eye doing so. Do I make myself clear? The prisoners are innocent. Jake knows one from his hometown." She narrowed her eyes, having never spoken to the boy this way. She was sure he understood the shaky spot he was in.

Can I trust Freddy? He'd been a pain in her side from the first day they'd met.

Adaline glanced up at Jake to find him looking at her as if the whole plan had just gone up in smoke. And in reality, it most likely had.

Chapter Twenty

Dalton stared at the bowl of beans and cornbread he held in his hands, and then wiped the sweat from his feverish forehead. An illness had gripped him last night, sapping the little strength he had left. Looking at the food in his bowl made his empty stomach pinch in on itself. This was the most he and Merryweather had been served since they'd arrived. Seemed the guards wanted them sated and drowsy when making the walk to the docks. After abstaining from eating his food for two and a half days, he was plenty hungry.

Activity up and down the harbor road had mesmerized him and Merryweather all day. He watched each wagon, buggy, or horse and rider to come their way. Time was running out. Buckboards transporting the bounty the *Tigress* had brought into port passed each other, the friendly shouts of greeting barely audible to Dalton's ears. He'd scanned every conveyance looking for *the girl*—wanting, needing to see her face—but the road was a fair piece away, making minor details like the features of a young woman difficult to see.

The aroma of pork chunks floating in sauce-covered beans made Dalton's stomach squeeze.

Maybe the men didn't drug the food. Maybe I can eat. Just this once. Just this once . . .

Dalton jerked his gaze away from his bowl before he tipped the whole thing into his mouth. Of course, they'd drugged it. They wouldn't chance him talking now.

He swallowed, looked off into the distance for a moment, and then turned away, intent on sticking with his plan, no matter how much he needed to eat. He took a small step toward the outhouse, hating what he was about to do. The guards were too intent on their own meal to notice him.

"Hold up, Number Three," the guard named Durst commanded, setting his spoon back into his bowl. "Get back over here and eat. Don't you know that's bad manners taking your supper to the other side of the yard?"

The guard named Rigley sneered as he gobbled down his meal.

When Dalton didn't respond fast enough, he saw Durst climb to his feet.

"You heard me. Don't start giving me trouble now, not unless you want to get roughed up before your boat ride north. That won't be no fun at all with the rough seas coming your way." His eyes narrowed and he set aside his bowl, resting his palm on the butt of his revolver. "Don't make me tell ya again."

Dalton shook his head. "My stomach's sour. I'm gettin' sick. I can't eat."

Durst pulled his gun from the holster. "You'll eat or I'll shoot ya, sour stomach or not."

As much as Dalton knew this would be the end of any kind of escape plan, he had no choice. He lifted his spoon, scooped in a mouthful, letting the warm sensation coat the inside of his mouth. The food was warm and tasty. Torn, he wanted to shovel it in, and yet he knew he shouldn't eat a bite.

"Swallow it."

Dalton's gaze landed on a funny-looking fellow scratching around the dirt, lifting rocks and examining each one before pitching them away. He'd been down by the tracks earlier, and Dalton hadn't noticed that he'd gotten so close, only about two end-to-end train cars away. The man's black Stetson was pulled down on his forehead and Dalton couldn't see his face, but something about the fellow looked familiar.

"Eat."

Dalton scooped up another spoonful, not taking his gaze off the man in the field.

Merryweather, already finished, slid his bowl under the bottom wire laid almost atop the ground. He belched and wiped his mouth with the back of his hand.

The guard gestured to Dalton's bowl with his gun barrel.

The move caused Dalton to scoop up another bite. Perhaps escape once they landed in Alaska might be possible. Before long the drugs would hit his empty stomach, and he'd be carried back to the haziness he'd left behind last Tuesday—but the beans and pork tasted good. Soon, he'd not be good to himself or anyone, but he'd still be alive. And as long as he was alive, he'd have the will to live. To escape. To take back his life.

Dalton scooped in another bite, now unable to stop his unruly hand. The damage was done. He was sure he'd wake up in the belly of some foul-smelling ship navigating the ocean.

His heart sank. Perhaps he'd never see Wyoming again, or Colorado, or his parents. Sadness stabbed inside, and then a wave of bliss washed over him. The drug was taking effect. As he swayed, he grasped a fence post. Just before he closed his eyes, he saw the face of the fellow working in the dirt. He'd come closer still and was looking directly at Dalton.

Shock clamored inside. He knew that face. Didn't he? But from where? He couldn't remember...

❀

A few minutes after the sun disappeared into the ocean, Adaline, wrapped in her wool cape with the hood pulled up over her head and a basket over her arm, walked toward home, the tickets she'd purchased with Jake's money deep in her skirt pocket. She'd waited until right before closing to go to the depot, hoping to avoid seeing anyone she knew.

Thoughts of Dalton Babcock, a man she'd never met, kept circling around in her mind. The way his eyes had narrowed when she'd sent the secret message. The dangerous feel of his presence. Jake must think highly of him to risk his own life. Especially when her brother had Daisy waiting for his return.

A smile tugged at her lips. Jake was a good man. She was so thrilled he'd been dropped into her and her sister's life, even if Courtney didn't realize her good fortune yet. She was too wrapped up with Wil and what would happen to their relationship once the trio moved away.

A night bird called, giving Adaline pause. The road was quiet and she pulled her cape closer around her shoulders, feeling alone. While she'd been at the depot, fog had moved in off the choppy sea and now thickly blanketed the ground. She could hear the distant crash of the waves against the rocks beyond the cliffs of the shoreline. She'd yet to see the *Tigress* but had admired the old, battered ship many times before.

She shivered. The thought of the poor souls who were stolen away from their families made her sick, and a cold chill ran up her back. Jake was right. This was dangerous business, not some silly game they were playing. Life was precious and could be lost in the blink of an eye.

She thought of the items in her basket. Some bread and cheese. Leftover roast. And hidden below a blue napkin laid at the bottom, two sets of her father's pants and two shirts. She planned to stash the basket outside somewhere she could get to it quickly once the dark of night had fallen.

Courtney and Mrs. Torry thought she had gone to the mercantile to help Mrs. Bennett with a few last projects, but in reality, she was putting into motion the plan she and Jake had worked out. He'd gone out much earlier, making some excuse that he had business to talk over with the banker about their father's possessions, when in reality he was procuring a wagon from the livery and a few other things.

The depot road that had been so busy earlier was now almost deserted. She walked alone in the shadows. If they were found out, would anyone else believe them? That the men weren't really convicted criminals? Would the town get behind her and Jake, or would they support Hexum?

Turning, she looked at the prison camp, now barely visible in the ever-darkening sky. She needed to get home. Several hours to wait still remained.

The sound of buggy wheels behind her made Adaline turn. Too far away to see the occupants, she stepped off the road, not wanting to be hit in the waning light and fog. The carriage loomed closer.

Hexum!

"Whoa," he called to his horse, stopping by Adaline's side. "What are you doing out here alone? It's late. This road isn't safe with all the seafaring men in port. Surely, you're smarter than that."

She bristled but didn't let her anger show. "I'm on my way home now."

He leaned over the seat and put out his hand. "Get in. I'll take you home. James hasn't been dead but a few days, and you're already into mischief. Has your half brother arrived? I haven't heard."

Adaline just stared at the man's hand, loath to touch it. But if she didn't, he might become suspicious. As long as he didn't question her about what she had in the basket, she'd be fine. She placed her palm in his, staying her reaction to shiver, and climbed into the rocking buggy, discreetly setting the basket by her feet.

"Well, what do you have to say for yourself, Adaline?" he repeated. "You've grown up here. You know sailors in their cups can be rambunctious."

Rambunctious? Just like Hexum to downplay the crimes some of the sailors committed against women. Now that she knew the banker had been blackmailing her at the same time he was hoodwinking her father, she hated him all the more. Having to answer galled her.

"The sunset caught me off guard, Mr. Hexum. I had business at the depot. I'm not but a few minutes away."

"Business?"

"Yes." She knew he was waiting for an answer, but she'd not give one.

"Do you always have to be so prickly? I'm only trying to help. You act as if I'm the enemy." He clucked to his horse and they started off.

Agitation at her father for telling Hexum about Jake rippled inside. They were turning onto Seashore Lane and would be at her house in only a few more minutes. Fearing the conversation would come back to Jake, and whether or not he'd arrived, she plastered on a pleasant smile.

"I'm sorry. I guess I am always a little offish to you, Mr. Hexum. I don't mean to be. The last few years have been difficult, and now . . ."

"Hugh. Call me Hugh."

"Yes, well, Hugh. This too shall pass." She didn't flinch when he reached over and laid a comforting hand on her arm. "What are you about tonight?" she asked pleasantly, wondering how he would answer. *Down at the docks seeing to your evil deeds?* "Were you at the depot as well? I didn't see you or your buggy."

They turned again. Her house was at the end of the road. They'd be there in moments.

"Uh, no. I was at the harbor. I'm sure you've heard the *Tigress* has finally arrived. I needed to speak with the captain. You know I have clients in Alaska. Wanted to make sure my last shipment of goods arrived to them safely."

When the buggy halted, she didn't wait for his answer or his help to descend to the street, but instead climbed out on her own.

Shipment of goods, all right. As in slaves for his mine.

She hurried to the door. "Thank you, *Hugh*," she called over her shoulder. "I appreciate the ride."

She hurried inside, thankful he'd not asked her any more questions. Not until she had gone into the bedroom she was sharing with Courtney and quietly closed the door did she realize she'd left the basket in his buggy.

Would he find it? Look through it? If he did, what would he think of the men's clothes clearly hidden under the food?

If they could just make it to seven o'clock tomorrow, after Dalton and the other man were on the train and well on their way to Logan Meadows, she'd breathe a sigh of relief.

Chapter Twenty-One

———❦———

Half past two in the morning, at the end of a deserted street, Jake carefully pulled the stick of dynamite from his saddlebag. He'd gotten the explosive from a gun shop, saying he'd found an area he thought might produce some bones. He smiled to himself, thinking, *What bone hunter would blow a hole into the earth?* But his answer had satisfied the man asking.

He glanced around, set the stick into an old log where the diversionary explosion wouldn't do any real damage to personal property, but would make a loud enough noise to cause confusion. The area wasn't far from the prison camp, so the guards would be curious. He attached the firing wire, carefully laying it out a good ten feet and clearing the land around with his cowboy boot to make certain the flame would burn to the explosive.

A growing sadness had been building inside him for the past few days. Why hadn't he said the words to his father? What could doing so hurt? Every time he closed his eyes, he saw James in the bedsheets as he'd been at his passing. He longed to be home again, pushing cattle, having supper at the Silky Hen, and sleeping in his bed in the bunkhouse.

Finished, he glanced up into the sky. Nothing would stop him from getting home. And once he got there, Jake was staying put—marrying Daisy—and starting his life over. Finding his father and sisters was worth the heartache, but now he was anxious to get back . . . and in one piece.

No time like the present. The plan was laid. Adaline was ready. He lit the fuse and ran to his horse, swung aboard, and galloped toward his destination.

KABOOM!

Jake felt the concussion of the blast on his back. Riding on, he finally reined up behind some trees and watched the prison compound, still too far away to see any details. Soon excited voices reached him. One guard mounted and rode away. Slipping off his horse, Jake carefully sprinted forward, thankful for the set of dark clothes Adaline had dug out of her father's things. He hovered behind the guard shack, pulled his gun, and when the remaining guard stepped within reach, Jake struck him over his head with the stock of his gun.

The man crumpled to the ground without making a sound.

Cupping his hands over his mouth, Jake gave a birdcall. Adaline had told him the men wore the key on a chain around their waist. Dragging the unconscious man over to the gate, Jake retrieved the key and after a few fumbling attempts, had the key in the lock.

Adaline suddenly appeared at his side. "Hurry. The other guard will be back soon."

Flinging open the gate, they rushed in and slid open the door to the train car to the gaping blackness.

"Wait here," he said to Adaline, not knowing what to expect. By feel, he found a sleeping Dalton and hauled the heavy man to his feet.

"Waah," he mumbled.

Jake felt heat radiating off his friend's face. "Dalton. Wake up." He roughly patted his cheeks.

"Where's the other one?" Adaline asked, having disobeyed and followed him inside.

"Over there. I have Dalton up; see if you can get the other fellow to his feet."

"I can't. He won't wake up."

"They've been drugged. Hold Dalton steady," Jake ordered.

Once Adaline had Dalton, Jake easily pulled up the small man, not that much larger than Adaline, and walked him through the door, and out the gate. He pushed the man's hands on the post and commanded him to stay. Running back inside for Dalton, he grasped his other side.

"Let's go. You go get the other prisoner, and I'll take care of our tracks." Slapping his friend's face, Jake said, "Dalton. You awake?"

"Waah," was Dalton's only response.

It felt like an hour had elapsed before Jake could get him outside. Somehow, Adaline kept both men on their feet as Jake grasped the hefty rock he'd brought along. He set it by the guard's head, to make it look as if one of the prisoners had somehow knocked him out. Breaking a branch from a shrub, he made fast work of sweeping away their evidence, and then threw the branch into the bushes.

"If we don't move right now, it's over."

Jake went first, dragging and pulling, working to keep Babcock on his feet as they stumbled down the hill in the darkness. He could hear Adaline's encouraging words behind as she assisted the other fellow. Jake had been so intent on getting away, he just now began to hear some of the commotion from town where he'd set off the diversion. A few more feet and they'd reach some cover, then several hundred feet past the trees was the buckboard.

They were headed four miles away to Yaquina Head lighthouse, where Adaline assured him a large pig shed stood vacant, no longer used by the keeper. They could drive the buckboard inside, where the wagon and the men would stay the rest of the night. They'd tend the men, change them into other clothes, then somehow get them on the train unseen. This idea was feeling crazier with each step Jake took.

He spotted the partially hidden wagon in the tiny glimmer of the crescent moon. "Over here. Behind the trees. Hurry."

He set both of Dalton's hands on the lowered tailgate, lifted one knee, and boosted him into the straw, face first. The man grunted and rolled over, staring at the sky, a funny smile on his face. Turning, Jake found Adaline directly behind, breathing heavily from the exertion. He took the man from her and repeated the process, covering them both with straw. Quickly taking the folded tarp from behind the wagon seat, they unwrapped it and covered everything.

"I'm going for Joker. I'll be back in five minutes. If I'm not—" Jake realized he was speaking to his sister's retreating back as she climbed onto the buckboard's seat.

She gathered the lines. "I'll go now, Jake. Take the old road. You catch up. I feel exposed out here, even though we're in the trees."

He didn't want her to go on unprotected, but she was right about waiting. They shouldn't be spotted anywhere near this place.

"This was a foolish idea. I don't know what I was thinking," he mumbled.

"I do. You're a good man. I like that about you. Now, go get your horse and meet me on the road."

Thank goodness Adaline was stubborn. He couldn't have pulled this off without her help. He watched her slap the lines over the geldings' backs, knowing they weren't out of trouble yet. Getting them—*all four of them*—out of this dangerous situation alive would be the most difficult task of all. And they'd have to stay hidden while doing it.

Chapter Twenty-Two

"Mr. Babcock can't make it, Jake. Not this morning. He's sick. He won't get more than a few steps at the train station, and someone will spot him."

With water from her canteen, Adaline gently bathed Dalton's sweaty face with the moist cut-away section of her petticoat. Protectiveness welled inside for the large man who, at the moment, was no stronger than a kitten as he lay in the back of the wagon, sheltered from sight in the pig shed.

"Take Mr. Merryweather on, and I'll stay here. It's better the two split up anyway. Strangely and his men will be looking for both escapees together."

Mr. Merryweather stood silently at Jake's side, trembling. He'd become more alert as the hours had passed. The quiet man had thanked them profusely for bringing him along when they busted out Dalton. He was now dressed in a suit of her father's best clothes, with a long black overcoat to cover up how large they were on him. He also wore one of her father's dapper hats.

Adaline's heart warmed. At least her father's belongings were being put to good use. No one would recognize the self-professed tailor as one of the escapees last seen in black-and-white stripes.

If he minded his own business, boarded the train quickly, took a seat, and then hid himself behind a newspaper, he should be fine.

"He have the grippe?" Jake asked, his expression dubious in the light of the one lamp they'd brought along as he stared at his sick friend. Looked as if more was on his mind than he was saying.

"I think so. His fever's very high. He's been delirious. I can't leave him alone. Here," she said, handing her bag over the wagon side. "The train tickets are inside. Take one for Mr. Merryweather and get moving if you don't want to miss the seven o'clock departure."

She gazed down into Dalton's sleeping face. He'd tossed and turned for hours once they arrived inside and closed the door. Until then, her heart had been wedged in her throat. "It's my guess Hexum will have a search party out, so be careful."

Jake just stood there.

"Go, Jake! Ride Mr. Merryweather double to the edge of town."

The man's broken glasses might be a problem. Although he was very common looking and would blend in with the morning crowd, his glasses weren't. The guards would see those right off.

"Don't forget to keep your glasses in your pocket, Mr. Merryweather," she said. Was Jake stalling because he didn't want to leave her alone? She'd have to be bossy to make him go. "Walk straight to the train and board directly. Don't talk to anyone, and don't tarry. Jake will get you there just before the train is ready to pull out."

Mr. Merryweather nodded, looking scared to death.

Jake's brows pulled down. "I don't feel right leaving you unprotected, Adaline. I'd figured on us staying together."

"There's no turning back now. Go, so you can come back tonight. By then, maybe he'll be better. This is the only way."

"How should I explain your absence to Courtney and Mrs. Torry?"

"That's easy. Tell them my friend Diana sent a telegram, and you drove me up to her house. Then you stayed over until this morning, and that I'll be back in a couple of days. She lives in the next town. They'll think me rude for not letting them know beforehand, but they'll believe you."

Jake went to the door and pushed it open an inch. "The place looks quiet."

"You best get moving. Once Malinda starts her chores around here, you'll be stuck until nightfall."

"No one will come in here?"

I hope not.

"No. The Plummers built a new shed on the other side of the barn. This one has been vacant for years." *The dust attests to that.* "We'll be fine. And even if they did, they're my friends. They'd never give me away. Go on, Jake. Now, while you still can."

※

All Jake wanted to do was get to Logan Meadows. Hold Daisy in his arms and kiss her sweet lips. He'd be a happy man to smell cow patties for the rest of his life, as well as fight the Wyoming cold once the snow started to fall.

Home was calling. He aimed to be there soon. Best to put his head into this storm and get it done—without getting caught.

With the way clear, he opened the door wide enough for his horse and quickly led him toward the trees. Poor Mr. Merryweather followed silently in his footsteps. Over the hours last night, he'd relayed how he'd been hit over the head when he went to put out his trash. He feared his employer in San

Francisco thought him irresponsible for running off. Thought he wouldn't have a job if he ever returned.

Jake led his horse deeper into the copse where they couldn't be seen from the lighthouse or the square, well-kept house that sat nearby. Mr. Merryweather stayed close on his heels.

The man's face had lost all color when they'd told him of their plans to take him back to town and put him on an outbound train. With no law to turn to, getting Jay Merryweather and Dalton away from the likes of Hexum and Strangely as soon as possible was vital. The captives could testify to Hexum's unlawful enterprise—but not if they were dead.

Jake mounted and stuck out his hand, helping the man aboard. "We'll go cross-country and come in on the back side of the depot. You have a ticket so you can just amble on." *Easier said than done.*

"Th-thank you," Merryweather stuttered, grasping the back of Jake's saddle. Joker danced nervously at the extra weight.

The wobbly response had Jake worried. "You'll do fine, Mr. Merryweather. Just stay the course. Have a reply ready if you're stopped and questioned. You were riding the train east. You got sick, had to get off in town, and took a room. You've been holed up until you felt better. Now you're moving on."

He felt the man nod as Joker picked his way through the off-road terrain. "Hexum broke the law. He and his men don't want to get caught any more than you want them to find you. Keep a level head and you'll do fine." *If they shoot at you, run like the devil.*

They rode in silence until they reached the end of the trees and had a view of the road leading to the depot.

"This is the end of the line." Reaching back, Jake took hold of Mr. Merryweather's arm and helped him down. "You remember what to say when you reach Logan Meadows?"

"I do. I'll go to the sheriff, Albert Preston, and tell him everything. That you couldn't send a telegram because the attendant could be in on the scheme. That if all went as planned, you and Dalton, as well as your sisters, should be on a train by the time I reach Logan Meadows."

Jake nodded. "That's right. He'll take over from there. I'm sure someone will lend you the money to travel back to San Francisco." Jake reached in his pocket and pulled out a dollar coin. "Sorry, but this is all I can spare. My money's runnin' low. If you're careful, you can make it last for the handful of days."

"Thank you, Jake. I surely appreciate all you've done. I can say without a doubt, you saved my life."

Jake brushed off the compliment. "You'd do the same." He took a moment to study the happenings at the depot. "I'll keep watch until the train departs." *Not that I'll be able to do much if something happens.*

He looked into the small man's eyes. "Good luck."

Chapter Twenty-Three

Adaline didn't have a watch, but she knew the hour must be close to three in the afternoon. Did Mr. Merryweather make his train? Had Jake been found out? She'd sneaked out of the pig shed just once to relieve her bladder, but other than that, she'd stayed in the wagon with Dalton, worrying over what might be happening in town, and about the health of the man beside her.

Kneeling in the straw, she withdrew a strip of meat from her pack and placed it between one of Mrs. Torry's biscuits. Chewing, she reclined against the sideboard staring at Dalton, who was still asleep.

He'd woken up a few times throughout the day, delirious. His anguished words had tugged at her heart.

Who was Dalton Babcock? What kind of a man was he? She liked his face, his strong, manly jaw now covered in thick, dark whiskers. His tanned skin attested he spent time outside. Doing what, she didn't know. Fine lines fanned away from the corners of both eyes, put there, she thought, from smiling.

His eyes came open, and his gaze slowly took in the dark rafters above his head. The spiderwebs and dust. Near her leg, his hand fisted in the straw.

"Hello," she said softly, not wanting to spook him. "How do you feel?"

His gaze moved to her face. "Groggy. Like I've been hit by a train, but lived to tell about it."

Seeing him swallow, she reached for her canteen and screwed off the lid. "Take a little water. You've been burning hot for hours. I'm glad you've finally woken up." She slipped her arm under his shoulders and gently lifted, putting the canteen to his lips. He was large. She had to struggle to keep the water from spilling. "Easy, not too much at once."

He took several large gulps and grasped for the canteen when she tried to take it away. "More," he rasped.

"In a minute. You don't want to overload your tender stomach. You've thrown up several times. Bile only, so I know there's not much inside you."

He was shaky and moved slowly as he lay back. "Who are you?"

"My name's Adaline Costner."

As recognition took hold, his eyes narrowed. "You're the girl who brought the food."

She nodded, pleased he'd remembered her. "That's right."

His eyes closed and he grimaced. The water was most likely making him feel sick.

"Why? How?" he struggled to get out. "I don't understand. You don't even know me."

"I do. You're Dalton Babcock."

Breathing through his mouth for several seconds, he finally opened his eyes. One side of his mouth pulled up. "Now you're just being mean." A teasing look appeared in his tawny-colored eyes, fringed with dark lashes.

Oh my, for a man to look at her like that should be against the law—as if they shared a secret, as if something was between them that no one else could ever know.

Adaline jerked away her gaze and a flash of awareness blazed through her body. She gathered her jittery nerves. This man could be dangerous to her heart. She'd never been in love before, so this heady, excited feeling was a totally new experience.

"I'm sorry. I didn't intend to be mean," she said softly. "You see, my brother is Jake Costner. He recognized you in the prisoner camp."

His brow crinkled. "Jake Costner?" he said slowly.

"Jake—from Logan Meadows."

He tried to angle up on an elbow, but she kept him down with the tip of a finger. Reaching to the front seat, she took her coat, rolled the garment, and placed it under Dalton's head.

"Thank you," he said. "Are you speaking of the Jake who works for Chase Logan?"

She smiled and nodded. Seemed the drugs in his system were almost gone. "Yes, one and the same."

"But from what I knew, that cowhand didn't have a last name. Everyone in town knew he was touchy over the matter. You say he's Jake Costner, your brother?" He rubbed a shaky hand across his face.

"My father's been gravely ill. In the little time he had left, he wanted to meet the son he'd sired but never seen. He sent for him. When Jake arrived in Newport, he spotted a felon in the wire compound who looked like a man he knew by the name of Dalton Babcock. He wanted to get closer, to see if he was right. When I wheedled out of him what he was thinking of doing, I tried to discourage him. I feared for his life. I didn't want to lose the brother I'd just discovered."

"That's when you came to the camp?"

She nodded. "I wanted to prove him wrong so he'd give up his foolish idea. Instead, your reaction to the town's name proved him right. I couldn't keep the information to myself. He was none too happy I had taken matters into my own hands, but at least he was sure then what he wanted to do."

Dalton rubbed a hand over his forehead. "That's some story." Suddenly, his expression fell and he looked around. "The other man?"

"You mean Jay Merryweather? Jake put him on today's eastbound train to Logan Meadows, or at least, that's what was supposed to happen. You were supposed to go too, but . . ."

"I got sick?"

She nodded.

"You've put yourself in a lot of danger, Miss Costner. Over someone you didn't even know."

"Jake thinks the world of you. He wouldn't leave you behind."

That brought a worried frown. "And your father?"

"He passed on."

Ever since her father was buried, she and Jake had been making plans for Dalton. She hadn't really taken any time to grieve. Now she felt as if she were drowning in the tears yet unshed. She sat silently, unable to think of anything to say.

Dalton reached out and touched her hand, the fever passing through his fingers. "I'm sorry. Having your pa pass on and putting yourself into danger must be hard. You're a very brave girl."

Adaline swiped away a tear sliding down her cheek. Dalton's soft, caring voice had called out her emotions. "Keeps my mind off him. And that he's gone. I'm worried now about Jake. He should have been back hours ago. I can't imagine what would keep him away unless the worst has happened."

"He's been delayed. Jake's a clever one. No one's gonna get the best of him."

That made her smile and look into his eyes. They held wisdom, warmth, and a whole lot of appeal. She needed to distract herself.

"Do you need to, ah—is nature calling at all?"

He chuckled. "Now that you mention it . . ."

She scooted through the straw to the end of the wagon and went to the door to peek out, see when it was clear so she could help Dalton outside to the bushes. The sight of Frank Plummer, the lighthouse keeper, walking their way with a bucket in hand, made her take a stumbling step back. The horses munching in the feed bags stopped and lifted their heads, ears forward.

"The light keeper is coming," she whispered frantically and glanced around. There was no time to hide. The large wagon, two horses, and a sick, escaped convict would be a mite difficult to explain.

Chapter Twenty-Four

Jake paced the kitchen floor, antsy to get back to the pig shed with news and food. Unfortunately, Wil Lemon had picked today to drop in on Courtney, and with Mrs. Torry visiting her sister, Jake didn't dare go off and leave the two alone in the house.

He glanced at the clock hanging above the sink. Only five minutes since the last time he'd looked. Adaline must be worried sick.

And how was Dalton? Had he gotten any better? The way he'd looked this morning, they'd be lucky to be on the outbound train by Wednesday. How would they keep him hidden, along with what they'd done to break the two men out? Each hour that passed, he expected someone to pound on the front door.

He glanced at the clock again. Half past six. How long before he could tell Lemon—politely, of course—to leave? This morning after Jake had returned, he had been making some headway with Courtney, and he didn't want to lose the valuable ground he'd gained by upsetting her. Her temperament was so different from Adaline's. He and his oldest sister seemed to think much the same. Sometimes she amazed him by saying things he was about to say himself.

Not so with Courtney. She was a mystery. Just when he thought he'd upset her, she'd give him an endearing glance. He had much to learn about women.

"Jake?" Courtney called, in between laughter coming from the front room for the last ten minutes. "Can you look at the teakettle for me, please? Is the water boiling?"

His eyebrows shot up as he turned to the stove. He'd never made a cup of tea in his life, but he could see the steam shooting from the kettle. Somehow, he felt he knew what would come next . . .

"Looks more than done," he called back, glancing then at the tray she'd set out, two teacups in saucers and a plate of cookies between. Just then the kettle began to whistle.

Courtney gave a small laugh.

"At least she's not crying anymore," Jake muttered under his breath, relieved she'd forgotten for a moment about their pa's passing. Maybe Lemon was good for something, albeit that was all.

"Oh, I hear it now," she said, sweetness dripping in her voice. "Would you mind adding the tea and pouring the water? Wil is in the middle of a funny story, and I don't want to interrupt him."

Jake would do anything for his sisters, but serving tea to a scoundrel like Lemon wasn't going to happen.

"Jake?"

Irritated, he stomped to the pantry where he'd seen Adaline and Courtney return with a bag of tea leaves. He glanced around. Agitated, he snapped, "Yes, I *would* mind. You come in here. Wil can just hold his thought."

A second later, Courtney appeared alongside him in the pantry. "He's just trying to cheer me up. I thought you'd at least understand that." She wedged in front of him and reached for the bag he'd been searching for.

He shifted his weight from one leg to the other, feeling the fool. "Maybe I do know that. But maybe I ain't never made a cup of tea before. We drink coffee in the bunkhouse, Courtney."

"Well, why didn't you just say so?" she replied in a clipped tone. "I don't want you taking on too much now. It might strain your brain."

"You hush. We're all a little off with your pa dying."

"Your pa too."

He shrugged. "How long is Wil planning to stay? I have things to do, and I'm not leaving you two alone."

She reared back as if that was the most horrible insult he could throw her way. "What are you thinking? Sakes alive, you sure have a low opinion of me."

Jake jerked his thumb over his shoulder, pointing to the parlor. "Not of you, of him. When did Mrs. Torry say she'd be home?"

"After church tomorrow."

"Tomorrow?" *What am I going to do about Adaline and Dalton?*

"Don't look so surprised. Tomorrow *is* Sunday, you know. And she usually doesn't come back until late Sunday afternoon. She's been working steady since Papa . . ."

Right there, standing in the pantry and arguing with his little sister, the reality of Jake's new situation almost knocked him over. He was a big brother. A *real* big brother. And his sisters were depending on him to keep them safe, whether they knew it or not. This close to Courtney, he could see the insecurity in her face she was trying so hard to hide.

"I guess it's about time I learned to make tea," he said softly, making her eyes widen in surprise. There wasn't anything he could do now for Adaline, but he could for Courtney. "Maybe when I get home, I can surprise Daisy by doing up a cup for her. We'll have to see."

A tiny smile curled Courtney's lips. "Maybe you can. Let me show you how. I think you'll be amazed at how easy it is—*even for a cowboy.*"

The warmth that infused the word "cowboy" had him blushing. Having sisters was turning out to be a treasured gift. The memory of his father engulfed in his bedding only moments before his death chased away the good feelings, and he straightened.

"Well, let's get to the task, if it's so easy."

As Courtney shook the tea from the crumpled brown sack, a loud knock sounded on the front door. The women who had come and gone of late leaving their respects, as well as a cooked dish, didn't knock like that.

Jake strode through the room before Lemon had a chance to stand and opened the door.

Hexum.

The crooked banker gave Jake an insolent stare. "I'd like to speak with Miss Costner—Adaline."

He doesn't recognize me. I must have been so beneath him the day I was in the sheriff's office, he never gave me a thought—or a look.

"She's not here," he replied, keeping a hold of the door. The last thing he needed was for the banker to come in. Every minute that passed was a chance for Jake to begin to look familiar.

Hexum's smile was malevolent. "Where is she?"

"Out of town." *Not that it's any of* your *business. I'll never let her marry the likes of you.*

"Out of town?"

"Visiting a friend."

Hexum's smile faded. "She didn't mention any of this to me. You must be her half brother."

Jake nodded. "That's right. Jake Costner. What can I do for you?" At that moment, he noticed the wicker basket at the man's feet.

Hexum followed his gaze. "I'm returning some belongings of hers she left in my buggy when I gave her a ride home yesterday evening."

Adaline had told him what she'd accidently done. She'd been very upset over her carelessness. Had Hexum found the clothes? The anger in his eyes said he had. Was this a game of cat and mouse? Who could outsmart whom?

Jake reached down and brought the basket inside. "I'll see that she gets it when she returns."

"When will that be?"

"Don't know."

When Hexum gazed past Jake's shoulder, recognition shone in his eyes. Lemon must have gotten up and come to see who was at the door.

"I hope she's being careful," the banker said. "In case you haven't heard, two escaped convicts are on the run. You best keep your doors locked. They're armed and dangerous. If you encounter them, shoot to kill."

Jake caught Hexum's gaze on his gun. Not surprising that the man would rather have Dalton and Merryweather dead so they couldn't spill the beans on him. "Shoot to kill? By whose order?"

"The United States Army."

"Mr. Hexum." Courtney had come into the room.

"How're you, Miss Costner?" His face took on a gentler expression. "My condolences about your father. I'm sorry I was unable to make the funeral."

"Thank you," she said. "Would you like to come in for a cup of tea?"

"No. I have pressing business."

Yeah, like finding the men who can expose your dirty little secret and killing them. Too bad for you one is already long gone.

Jake watched the interaction. The sooner he could put Dalton on a train, the better. Clues were out there for the finding, like the buckboard, and the dynamite he'd said he needed for excavation. Sooner or later, someone would put two and two together. By then, he wanted to be on the eastbound train himself.

Chapter Twenty-Five

The shed door crackled and popped, the sharp sound snapping through the shadowy space. Adaline swung around, pushing away her fear and hoping Jake had finally returned. But no, just a stiff gust of wind off the ocean from the blustery storm outside. The building rattled and groaned. Adaline prayed it wouldn't fall down around their ears.

She wrapped her arms around herself and resumed her pacing. The last time she'd looked outside, the night was pitch dark except for the light beaming from the lighthouse out to sea.

Where was Jake? Mr. Plummer had come so close to discovering them earlier in the day, she'd almost fainted. Looked as if she and Dalton would be passing the evening alone. Had Hexum and Strangely put two and two together? Did someone see Jake lighting the dynamite and turn him in to the guards? A hundred different things could have happened. Was he hurt? Did he need her?

She glanced up into the wagon bed where Dalton dozed through the storm. Around midday, he'd seemed like he was on the mend, but as the hour grew late and the sun went down, his fever had climbed again, and he had a bad headache. He'd need something to eat soon. A weak chicken broth that he'd be able to keep down would do him a world of good.

A gust hit the end of the building and one of the geldings snorted. Since the wind had picked up, they were fidgety, spooky. Their wide eyes put her on edge.

They'd need water tonight. Adaline had drained the canteens for them except for a small amount she kept back for Dalton. After nightfall, she'd have to sneak out. Find water. She didn't dare lead the horses out. Expecting to have both men on the train, and be home by now, she and Jake hadn't planned for a longer stay. She'd rationed, but now barely a handful of oats remained. Too bad horses didn't eat straw.

Nervous energy made her swallow. She was hungry too, but didn't dare eat the one remaining apple or either of the last two biscuits. Jake would come. She'd have faith. She couldn't give up hope.

"Miss..."

Dalton's raspy whisper reached her ears. Turning, she hurried to his side. "What is it? Are you going to be sick?"

He barely moved his head back and forth. "You can't stay here any longer. It's too dangerous. Those guards are searching for me. If they find us, you'll be in trouble too."

"We're four miles away, Mr. Babcock. Besides, *they* broke the law. Not me, and not you."

"There's no one here to take our side," he said slowly. "They've established themselves as reputable and will be shooting to kill, if they can. At least me. Maybe you, as well. I don't want to risk that. Can you find your way home on your own? Something must have happened to Jake."

The wind whistled around the shack, pulling at the shingles on the roof.

"I'm not leaving you. It's late now anyway. No one will come out in this storm. For now, I think we're safe."

He swallowed, pressing his lips tight.

Adaline hugged herself, feeling useless. "I wish I had some sodium bicarbonate to settle your stomach. How do you feel?"

"I'll live." He took stock for a long time before saying, "But you're dead tired. You need rest. I don't care if it's not proper—climb up into this straw and lay down beside me."

"I have to get water for the horses. I only have a little left for you."

"Give them each a handful. Do you have that?"

"I think so."

After she'd done what he'd said, he scooted from the middle of the wagon bed and patted the straw.

She couldn't stop her gaze from admiring the soft-looking resting place. How she'd love to sleep. She'd spent most the day peeking out the door, pacing, or slumping on the rock-hard seat.

"Come on," he coaxed. "Just rest for a few minutes."

At the sight of his raised brows and the edges of his lips pulling up, she nodded. Using the stool she'd found in the corner of the shed, she crawled up the tailgate. On hands and knees, she moved forward. Outside, the wind blustered. When she lay down, she pillowed her head on her arm, facing him.

He smiled. "Good girl."

The straw was as soft as she'd imagined. "Where're you from, Mr. Babcock?" she asked quietly. The smile was back in his eyes.

"Call me Dalton. And I'm from Colorado."

She thought about that for a minute. "And you should call me Adaline."

"Close your eyes. You're safe."

They *were* warm and safe, at least for the moment, Adaline realized. Taking a deep breath, she gazed into Dalton's eyes, no more than a foot in front of her face. His lids drooped—probably just to entice her to do the same.

She started to smile and he gave her a pointed look. Adaline let go of her fears and closed her eyes. Nothing was going to happen in the next few minutes. She'd rest now so she'd be able to keep watch as the night progressed.

Safe, her mind whispered. Safe and warm . . .

Dalton opened his eyes to the sound of the horses' hooves pawing the earth in the midst of a howling wind. A smattering of rain riddled the rooftop. The horses needed water and had grown restless. He wondered if he should just release them outside and let them find a creek on their own. But if later, they needed to move the wagon, they'd be stuck.

He looked over at Adaline and his heart swelled. She was young. Brave. Pushing away the fact she was pretty as well, he recalled the way she'd appeared when she'd come into the prisoner camp carrying the box of food. Now that he knew her, he recognized the secretive smile she'd worn the day when she'd been tricking the guards. How she'd boldly stared at him and Jay when she spoke her furtive code. If she wasn't asleep and he didn't want to wake her, he'd chuckle.

Still feeling weak, he lifted a hand out before his eyes to find it steady. He'd go in search of water. If this was a hog shed, there had to be other livestock around somewhere on the premises. How hard would it be to find a bucket and water trough?

Dalton carefully levered himself on his arm and slowly crept to the open tailgate. For a moment, his head swam in wooziness.

He stilled, waited for the sensation to pass. Once he felt better, he lowered one foot onto the stool and stepped onto the hard-packed earth, keeping a tight grip on the sideboard. He stood for several minutes, firming his legs under him, and drawing the attention of the two horses.

He was weak. No denying. But he'd been sick before. He'd push through this to get Adaline back to safety, if nothing else.

Glancing around, he spotted a man's coat on the wagon seat. Moving quietly, he retrieved the garment and slipped in his arms. Ready or not, he had a mission. He needed to get the chore done before Jake's sister woke up. If that happened, she'd never let him go.

With the coat buttoned up to his chin, Dalton wished for his black Stetson. The rain was pelting the ground and he was sure to be drenched by the time he returned.

Sliding the long door open only far enough to slip out, he stepped into the dark night, the wind and rain buffeting his face. The saltiness of the air stung his skin. Quickly, he slid the door closed and took stock of the dark surroundings.

Chapter Twenty-Six

Half past eleven and Jake lay awake atop his bed, still dressed and boots on, cursing himself for landing in this position. Adaline was never far from his thoughts. Fear for her kept him on edge. He didn't begrudge Mrs. Torry time off, but her visit couldn't have come at a worse time.

What was happening at Yaquina Head? Where were Hexum and his henchmen? If Jake didn't have Courtney to watch over, he'd already be out at the lighthouse and moving Dalton somewhere closer to the train depot where they could easily get him onboard.

His stomach gurgled. Anxiety had kept him from eating anything at suppertime. Swinging his legs over the bed, he headed for the kitchen and the many dishes the good people of Newport had dropped off. In the dark, he crossed from the hall to the far counter and felt around for the matches as he heard a sound. A muffled voice. A low moan.

Stricken, he turned his head, hoping the sounds were just his imagination. Wil Lemon had finally left around seven, plenty late, according to how Jake felt. The two had whispered their good-byes at the door for a good twenty minutes. Now a cold, hard fear had him striding to the front room.

Another almost indistinguishable sigh ratcheted up Jake's anger. No refuting what was happening on the settee. The two didn't even know he was there when, in a blinding fury, he grasped Lemon by the back of his shirt, pulled him off his sister, and threw him to the floor.

Courtney screeched out in fear, and Lemon scrambled to his feet.

"You stinking dog!" Jake roared after he drilled his fist into Lemon's face.

The man reeled backward, falling into a side table. Objects clattered to the floor.

"I'll kill you, you son—" Jake took an unexpected fist in the face, cutting off his sentence. The pain actually felt good in his state of mind.

"Jake, stop!" Courtney screamed. "Wil, please, stop!"

Jake wasn't stopping, and he was sure Lemon wouldn't either. The two had been circling this since the day they'd met. Sizing each other up, weighing their odds, anticipating the fight to come. Jake had believed Lemon was too old and rough for Courtney, and surely had only one thing on his mind. Unfortunately, the scoundrel had proved Jake right.

Seeing was difficult, but moonlight through the front window and Lemon's white shirt helped. The man lunged and Jake stepped aside, letting him fall to the floor.

Launching atop him, Jake pummeled the man's sides and face as fast as he could move. Lemon was large and heavy. If he ever got the upper hand, Jake might be in trouble. Jake had had surprise on his side. Now his anger wouldn't let Lemon beat him.

They rolled to the side, and from somewhere, he could hear Courtney crying. Begging for them to stop. Pleading, promising anything and everything.

Lemon smacked his forehead against Jake's jaw, sending a slicing bolt of pain through his face. Momentarily disjointed, he fell when Lemon shook him off. Not waiting an instant, Jake rolled and sprang to his feet, all the while dodging and ducking Lemon's fists.

Courtney screamed. That was when Jake saw a wicked-looking blade in Lemon's clenched fist. The man slashed out, a killing lust making his eyes glow.

Breathing heavily, Jake ducked. In the saloon, he'd seen a man carved to within an inch of his life before anyone could stop the brawl, and it wasn't a pretty sight. Lemon was out to kill.

"You've taken on the wrong man, cowpoke." Lemon laughed evilly. "I'll enjoy watching you die."

Courtney screeched at the top of her lungs and grasped his arm. Lemon knocked her back and sprang forward, aiming for Jake's throat.

Lightning fast and with all his strength, Jake batted Lemon's arm to the side. The back of Lemon's wrist struck the door frame. Using that moment of surprise, Jake hooked Lemon's leg with his own and tripped him. The scoundrel swayed and Jake landed another blow. A loud crack sounded when he felt the bones in Lemon's nose give way.

The man roared in pain, and the knife clattered to the floor.

Jake lunged forward with a shoulder, catching Lemon in the gut. The two fell to the floor and rolled across the room. Jake threw Lemon up against the opposite wall, beating the man's face and torso until his arms ached. Unconscious, Lemon slouched down the wall.

Jake hauled him up and carried him to the door by the back of his shirt and pants. After tossing him out, Jake locked the door. He limped into the kitchen. Finding the matches he'd been looking for before the trouble started, he had difficulty striking the coarse lighting strip.

On the third attempt, he had the match burning and touched the flame to the wick. Hearing Courtney's soft cries, he turned, seeing her for the first time in the light of the kitchen lamp.

He was angry. Furious. But his heart swayed. Not with wrath, but regret, love, loss.

Courtney's hair lay tangled around her shoulders and she gripped the front of her dress closed. No telling if the worst had already happened. He didn't think so because of Lemon's full state of dress, but Jake couldn't be sure. Her downcast gaze stayed on the floor, and her teeth chattered so loudly he could hear them from across the room.

Damn. He wanted to yell at her for letting Lemon back in the house. What was he supposed to say now? He had nothing. The situation was out of his realm of experience.

"Courtney," he finally said in a low voice, testing his jaw with his fingers. Warm blood trickled down the side of his face. "Courtney, what were you thinking? Why didn't you listen to me? To your pa?"

She only shrugged and kept her attention on the floor at his feet.

What good would talking do now?

"I'm sorry," she said in a small voice, finally stepping toward him. "I didn't think. Please, let me help you."

Her lips wobbled as her gaze caressed his face. Even in the dim light, Jake noticed the purple mark on her neck left behind by Lemon.

Hurrying away, she returned with a face cloth, her dress buttoned up. She worked the pump handle until water came forth and wet the fabric. After directing him to a chair at the table, she began to gently clean away the blood from his face.

Jake was thankful she was nursing him. He didn't know what to say, or do. At least this way, they were getting through the awkward minutes without having to speak. He wished Adaline was here. Or Daisy, or Jessie. A woman who would know what to do, what to say. Should he scold her or hold her? He'd never even contemplated such a moment, let alone lived through one.

"There. Stay put while I go get our medical box. I want to put gauze on the cut—"

Her breath hitched, and Jake glanced up to see her eyes glassy with tears. When one trickled down her cheek, she hurried away, only to reappear a moment later. She held a soft piece of fabric under his left eye.

"Can you please hold this?" she asked in a shaky voice.

Lifting his hand, he did her bidding.

"Let me see your knuckles."

"They're fine."

Jake stared across the room at a spot on the wall, embarrassed for her and angry too. Mostly, he wished he would have killed Lemon then and there when he had the chance, his own future be damned.

In her silence, he raised his gaze to hers. How she could even see for the amount of tears shimmering in her eyes, he didn't know. He stood slowly and held out his free arm as he kept the cloth pressed to the cut under his eye with his other hand.

Courtney stepped into his embrace, shaking uncontrollably. A soft sob escaped her throat when his arm closed around her, and then she really let her tears flow. She cried for several minutes.

She felt so small, so wounded. Her head pillowed on his chest. He was her brother, and he'd protect her to the ends of the earth.

"I'm sorry, Jake," she whispered without moving. "I didn't mean for anything to happen. It just did and—"

"Shh, honey." He stroked the back of her hair. "You don't need to say anything. I know you're sorry. I know that's not what you had in mind." *I hope it's not what I'm thinking.*

Her head wagged back and forth. "I don't want you to tell Adaline. Or Daisy either."

"It helps to talk with someone—you know, another woman." *Someone other than me. Someone who knows what to say.*

She pulled back and looked into his face, the weight of the world reflected in her eyes. "No. Adaline's always the good one and I'm always the bad one. I don't know why, but it's true."

He knew that feeling only too well. "You don't have to compare yourself with Adaline," he replied softly. "You don't have to compare yourself to anyone. You are who you are—a very special girl."

A girl. A young girl who doesn't need a snake like Lemon messing up your life.

Jake was feeling his way, hoping to say the right thing. He'd been about her age when he left Valley Springs and ventured with Chase and Jessie to Logan Meadows. He'd been wild and excited for the adventure, but for Courtney, leaving her home must feel frightening.

"Please, Jake? Promise me you won't tell a soul."

"I won't if you don't want me to."

"I don't."

"What happened tonight is just between us." *And Wil Lemon.*

"Thank you," she whispered. "I promise I won't let you down anymore."

He tipped her face up with one finger to see her sorrow. And a whole lot more. A life of never measuring up, of living in her sister's shadow, of letting people down.

Her brow crinkled. "What's life like in Logan Meadows?"

"Does this mean you're coming along?"

She swallowed and nodded. "I guess I will."

"Why now?"

She trembled and hugged him close, putting her face back against his shirt. The gesture made his heart constrict.

"Because Wil would have killed you tonight if you hadn't stopped him. Knifed you dead for protecting your sister. Papa was right about him. I couldn't have lived with myself if he'd killed you, Jake." She sniffed and leaned back again, searching his face. "Still, I'm scared of leaving. Where will I live? What will I do?"

A wave of thankfulness washed over him. She'd finally seen the light. A few cuts and bruises were definitely worth that.

"I'm thinking at first, both you and Adaline will live out at the ranch where I work. I'm sure Chase and Jessie will be pleased to have you. They have room. Then, if Adaline wants to live closer to town and get a job, she can live with my friend, Mrs. Hollyhock."

"That's a silly name."

Jake nodded. "I used to think that too when I was a boy. She's an old woman now, but she practically raised me. I owe her a lot. She'd give me her left arm, if I was to ask. I'd like to think Adaline could help her as she's growing older. Make her life a little easier. That might work out well."

"I want to work too, Jake."

"You will. But you have to finish school first. You can ride in and out of town with whoever takes Sarah into school, either me, Gabe, or Chase. The year will go by fast and before you know it, you'll be working or marrying and—"

What was he thinking, saying something like that? Did he want to send her back into Wil Lemon's arms?

As if knowing what he was thinking, a small smile appeared on her face. "You don't have to worry about me anymore. I've learned my lesson."

Reaching up, she'd covered the mark Lemon had left on her neck. She must have looked in the mirror when she went for the gauze. Did she have more experience than he realized? For now, she thought she didn't want any part of Wil Lemon. In the shame of her actions, she'd most likely say anything.

Wait until the two came face-to-face again. Would she still want to leave her home for Logan Meadows? Or would she fall back into his arms?

She stared at Jake for a long time. "I might be with child."

He fisted a hand, fighting back his urge to curse. He knew well the hardships she was in for if that were true.

"Either way," he said, tamping back his anger. His feelings wouldn't do a bit of good now. "You're better off without him. You have me and Adaline. We'll take care of you."

She nodded.

"He's gonna be mighty upset. He'll pressure you. Want you back."

"I know."

Jake glanced to the clock on the wall, thinking. "I'd like to avoid any more trouble. I think it best we leave Newport as soon as possible."

Her sad gaze went to the darkness outside the kitchen window.

Was she thinking of Lemon already? How soon would it be before the libertine came calling?

"When will that be, Jake?" she asked in a small voice. "I'll be ready."

"Just as soon as I can make it happen."

Chapter Twenty-Seven

A crowing rooster jolted Adaline out of her sleep. She opened her eyes and blinked, not recognizing the ceiling above her head. Actually, it wasn't a ceiling at all, but dusty wood covered in spiderwebs.

Repulsed, she went to sit up but remembered Dalton and turned her head. His side of the wagon was empty. The horses stared at her from their small enclosure a few feet away.

Dalton. Water. What was the time?

Daylight streaming through the cracks of the building sent fear up her spine. Jake hadn't returned, and now Dalton was gone. She scrambled down and went to the shed door, fearful of what she might see.

The rain had stopped. The ground was drenched, and large white clouds filled the sky for as much of the horizon as she could see. She'd have to go in search. Had someone come in and taken him? Surely not. She'd wake up, wouldn't she?

She patted down her rumpled clothes and tried to smooth her hair, pulling out strands of straw. The way looked clear, so she pulled open the door, stepped out, and closed it, the horses giving a soft whinny.

"Shh, I'll be right back, horses," she whispered, more to ease her own nerves. She felt bad for them, but she needed to find Dalton directly.

Staying low to the ground, she circled the homestead area, then followed the trees to the cliff. Looking down, she was relieved she didn't see anything, particularly a body lying on the rocks. That's not to say he still couldn't have fallen in the dark and washed out to sea.

She pushed the morbid picture from her mind and sneaked up to the new hog shed and yard. Several large animals looked up from their feed troughs. Someone had already been out here. She had to be careful. She didn't want to lie to Malinda or Frank if she were caught creeping around their place at daybreak.

A bucket, down by the gate. Staying low, she grasped the rope handle and started for the back of the barn. Maybe she could get inside without being seen. Carefully opening the door, she stepped inside. A handful of chickens pecked undisturbed at some scratch they'd been thrown.

"Adaline?"

Dalton?

She glanced up. Dalton was in the loft, staring down.

"Wait there," he said, moving toward the ladder. It took longer than it should for him to get down.

"What in the world were you doing up in the hayloft? I've been sick with worry."

"I went out to get water for the horses and almost got caught by a man, the light keeper, I think."

"You climbed the ladder by yourself?"

"Faster than a scared rabbit."

She let out a low laugh. He looked bedraggled, and she wondered what he would look like after a bath and a shave. The thought was intriguing.

"Well, I'm happy to hear that. No telling what the guards have been spreading around about you." She placed her hand on his forehead. "You're still hot, but not like yesterday. We need to get you back to the shed so I can water the horses." She lifted the bucket.

"Sorry. I guess I wasn't much help."

"I'm mad at you for even attempting something so foolish. You could have passed out in the rain. Who's to say you won't come down with a relapse?"

She started for the back door, glanced out a crack, and then turned to Dalton, who'd followed. "If Jake doesn't return this morning, I'll have to leave you alone and go see what I can find out. I still have two train tickets in my bag. We'll clean you up the best we can and get you ready in case you need to make a run for the train on your own while I'm gone. Do you think you'll have the strength to sit up today?"

"I climbed into a loft."

"Good enough, then let's go."

Adaline pulled up short. Two riders she recognized all too well were descending the road toward the lighthouse yard.

"The guards!" She yelped and flattened herself against the side of the barn as the men rode closer. "What should we do? We can't stay here. They'll search the barn and house. We need to make a run for it. Out back and into the trees. Do you think you can?"

Dalton's head was tipped back against the whitewashed wood. He still looked very weak.

"Do I have a choice?"

"No."

"Then what are we waiting for?"

Indeed, what? Those men wanted Dalton dead. And her too, she was sure.

Adaline took one moment to gaze into his eyes. Life was a mystery. Only a month ago, she was sadly going about her days with the heavy cloud of her father's impending death hanging over her head.

She closed her eyes and sent up a quick silent prayer. Perhaps today, she'd join him in heaven. "Not a thing. Let's go."

Chapter Twenty-Eight

Jake arrived at Yaquina Head as soon as darkness had fallen. The yard around the white clapboard house was quiet, and the flame in the lighthouse had yet to be lit.

Mrs. Torry had finally returned at six in the evening, leaving him free to get back to the abandoned pig shed. She'd been wide-eyed with fright at the prospect of encountering the escaped prisoners. As much as Jake had wanted to tell her and Courtney the truth, he didn't. For their own protection.

Courtney had been quiet all day, not saying more than a few words since the encounter with Lemon the night before. Jake had told her and Mrs. Torry he was going to speak with the preacher, who had offered to do a few things for them when the time arrived to leave.

That part was true. The fewer people who knew what was happening, the better. And he *had* stopped in at the parsonage for a few short minutes since Reverend Hensley was the only man in town Jake trusted. Then he'd ridden straight out here, keeping out of sight and avoiding the streets where suspicious gazes kept watch for the fugitives.

As soon as Jake arrived, he sensed the emptiness of the shed. The horses were the only living things inside. What had happened? Where had Dalton and Adaline gone? He moved quickly, gathering Adaline's things and stuffing them into his saddlebags. The one silver lining to this dangerous plan was Jay Merryweather was already on his way to Logan Meadows. Nothing could stop him now.

Where were Adaline and Dalton? Had they sneaked out, leaving the agitated horses? Or had they been discovered by Strangely and the guards? If so, he'd have to find them and then devise a plan to get them back and onto the train. This wasn't just some Sunday parlor game. Lives were on the line.

Jake swiftly harnessed the horses. He'd told the livery owner he'd have the rig and animals back on Monday, but he'd take them by the livery tonight and put them in the pasture after he returned the conveyance to its rightful spot. He didn't want it connected with the Costner house. He'd told the livery man he needed the wagon for his excavations. Luckily, a stream ran along the route to Newport where the horses could drink their fill. They looked hungry and thirsty.

With Joker tied to the tailgate, Jake waited for the moon to move behind the clouds to make his escape.

He fingered the sensitive spot under his eye, thinking about Courtney and how her life would change if she turned up with child. People could be cruel. One thing he knew—whatever was ahead, they'd face it as a family. She wasn't in this alone.

❁

Dalton kept watch on his feet so he wouldn't stumble as Adaline led him through the coastal shrubbery. He'd told her he was fine, when in reality, his head was swimming just as if he were out there in the big blue ocean treading water. With the way he felt, progress had been slow, and the day had ebbed away to darkness.

Jake's sister forged ahead like a warrior princess, unafraid of what they might encounter in the next few moments. This morning, when she'd spotted the guards riding for the lighthouse yard, she'd quickly taken stock of their surroundings and had them scrambling over loose rock and shale behind the barn pasture, his hand held firmly in her own. If only he didn't feel so rotten. And he had his guns. He'd dropped weight and strength since he'd been shanghaied in San Francisco, leaving him feeling like a different man.

"I wonder what Mrs. Landers thought when I never came back to my room?" he mumbled to himself. Heat radiated from his face, and his shirt clung to his moist chest.

Adaline kept moving. "Did you say something, Dalton?" she asked over her shoulder. "I didn't hear you."

"Wondering what my landlady did with all my belongings when I never returned."

Adaline stopped and turned. Her eyes went wide. "You're worse. I'm sorry. I shouldn't have pressed you so hard." She gazed around. "Here. Sit on this rock. If only I had my canteen. Do you want me to find a stream?"

He swallowed the best he could and shook his head.

She heaved a deep sigh. "I'll get you somewhere where you can lie down." Her expression was too confident. "Will you be all right here if I sneak up to the edge of the bushes and check the road to see if the way is clear? You need a few minutes to rest."

With her help, Dalton slowly lowered himself to the flat top of a large rock, the urge to throw up strong. "Sorry to slow you down," he mumbled. His mouth felt as if it were full of marbles. "It's taken hours just to come a few miles."

"Nonsense. We're practically in Newport. The town is just over the hill. I didn't want to run into those men, so I took the long way. I wonder if they searched the pig shed. If they did, by now they've found the wagon. They'll trace it to Jake, and from Jake to me, so I can't take you home. I'll have to think of somewhere to hide you."

The ground spun beneath Dalton's feet, and he wished he could help this girl in some way. She was shouldering all the weight.

Adaline jerked straight.

"What?" he mumbled.

"I have an idea. But you'll have to stay here alone for a little while. It's dark, and you should be safe. Can you do that?"

What choice did he have? He nodded. "But I don't want you taking any chances. If you get caught now, you'll be in real trouble. I don't know what Jake was thinking to let you do all this."

"Hush. He didn't have a choice." She glanced around one more time, gave him a satisfied nod he could barely see in the darkness, and then disappeared.

Within moments, the sound of her footsteps vanished, and all he could hear was the sound of the ocean waves breaking on the sandy beach somewhere off in the distance.

Chapter Twenty-Nine

At eight o'clock Sunday night, Jake heard the rattle of the front door key. Sick with worry, he strode across the room, quiet except for the tick-tock of the clock on the wall. He jerked the door open, ready to face whoever was outside, but praying for Adaline.

When he saw her face, a gush of relief spilled out. He pulled her inside. *She's alive.*

"Where have you been?" he barked out, unable to keep his agitation inside a moment longer. "I've been worried sick."

She tipped her head to the side and laughed, her disheveled appearance almost making him smile.

"Nice to see you too, brother." Her eyes went wide when she saw the cut under his left eye and the bruise on his chin. "What happened to you? Hexum's men?"

"No. Wil Lemon and I had a small disagreement."

"Oh no. What about?"

"Do we need a reason?" He'd told Courtney he'd have to give some reason when Adaline and Mrs. Torry saw his face. A fight over nothing was easy to believe. "Where's Dalton?"

She glanced around and then led him upstairs to the empty second floor. She held her finger to her lips until she was sure they were completely alone.

Jake narrowed his gaze to take in her appearance. She was not only filthy and her dress ripped, but lines of fatigue fanned out from her eyes and mouth, marring her usually perfect skin. Her eyes fairly drooped at half-mast.

"Safe for now. I had to move him."

"I know. I've been to the shed and retrieved the wagon and horses. Where is he?"

"You wouldn't believe me if I told you."

"Try me."

"Freddy's tree house at the back of his yard. It's set a good forty feet from the house, which is above the mercantile. I was careful getting him inside. No one saw us."

"What about Freddy?"

She rolled her eyes. "I don't know. I just hope he doesn't decide to go climbing in his tree anytime soon. If he does, at least he'll know who the visitor is and what we're up to."

This was risky. Jake didn't want to get Dalton killed in an attempt to save him from a life in Alaska, and that was exactly what would happen if Hexum and his men discovered the hideout.

"We need to get him on the train tomorrow."

"He can't, Jake. He's still so sick. And after traipsing around today, he's weaker than ever. He needs a few days. And by then, people will have let down their guard, thinking the convicts are good and gone."

"I don't like it. Someone will put two and two together pretty soon. Hexum brought back your basket."

Her mouth dropped open.

"The clothes were still inside."

"Maybe he's waiting for us to make a mistake."

"Could be. There's no way of telling. Is there a roof over Dalton's head in case of rain?"

"Yes, there's also a pallet and some old blankets. It'll be cold, but not much more than the shed had been. I can take him out more blankets, another coat, food and water. The location will have to do until he's well enough to board the train. We can't bring him here, although I'd like to." She glanced at her father's empty bed. "Only a matter of time before someone comes looking."

Jake reached out and ran a hand down Adaline's arm. This girl had guts. He couldn't ask for a better sister. Thoughts of Courtney filled his mind too, warming his heart. They'd get through these trials and make it home to Logan Meadows. And they'd accomplish the feat without anyone getting hurt or killed. Daisy was waiting.

"What about the horses and buckboard?"

"I returned them to the livery and turned the horses out into the pasture. I'll stop by tomorrow and explain I didn't need the wagon for as long as I thought."

"Was anything in the shed disturbed? Do you think the guards looked inside?"

"That's difficult to say. Nothing that I could tell was out of place. They were pretty lazy men."

"And dense."

He nodded. "Maybe they passed by."

"We can only hope."

Jake didn't want to stay in Oregon any longer than they had to. With Hexum and his men, and now Wil Lemon surely out to kill him, the sooner they skedaddled, the better. "I'll help you get those things together and take them out to Dalton."

"You don't know—"

"I'll find it. You're hitting the sack and getting some rest."

Adaline's face softened. "How's Courtney? Is she still set against leaving? I don't know how we'll get her on the train."

Again, a rush of love moved through Jake at the mention of his little sister. He felt he understood her now much better. "She's all right. I don't think she'll put up a fuss when we decide to go."

Almost out the door, Adaline swung around and looked him in the eye. "That's good to hear. But why? What changed her mind? She was so dead set against the move before."

Feeling protective, Jake shrugged. He'd never break his younger sister's trust. Everyone had events in their past they regretted. By going to Logan Meadows to make a new life, that was exactly what she'd do if she left her past here.

"I think she's ready to put all of the pain of James's death behind her and wants a new start. I can't blame her for that."

Adaline's gaze grew worried as she shook her head in agreement. "What about Wil? She was so set on marrying him. I wonder if something happened between them."

Jake chuckled to lead her away from the truth. "Let's concentrate on one problem at a time." He looked at the boxes of clothes they still needed to take to the church. "I'll find some warm things for Dalton. You clean up before Courtney or Mrs. Torry sees you and gets suspicious. And then get something to eat after you fix a box for Dalton."

Adaline gave a heavy sigh. "That sounds good. I'll have the food ready in ten minutes."

Jake nodded. "Let's get this done."

Chapter Thirty

Dalton reclined on the small pallet of his new hideout, thoughts of Adaline Costner floating through his mind. The tree house was strong, consisting of one small rectangular platform attached to a tall old oak surrounded by forest. Four walls held up a roof of sorts, and a sturdy rope tied to a thick branch extended to the ground and looked as if it could bear a man's weight.

Adaline had gone to pull the line up, but he'd stopped her. Anything looking different would create suspicion. The rickety slats of wood nailed to the slanting trunk had given him pause, but they'd held. The door was so small, he'd had to crawl inside. There were two windows.

An hour had passed since Adaline left him, promising to return with supplies and more blankets. He shivered from the cold, although he could tell his fever had climbed. The pallet swayed, or was that just the constant dizziness in his head? He was weak and his head ached. For some reason, up here in these branches, with an ocean breeze moving through the small windows, Dalton felt protected. This was a good hideaway. A place he wouldn't be discovered. At least, he hoped that was the case.

A soft rustle of someone walking stealthily caught his attention. Adaline? If it wasn't her, then he was in trouble. He listened as the person climbed the trunk, hand over hand. He had no weapon. Even if he did, he'd be hard-pressed to wield it.

"Dalton?" The voice was low, secretive.

Jake. During the escape Dalton had been drugged, and then delirious. He'd yet to speak with his friend.

Jake crawled through the opening, then turned and pulled in a heavy sack. Moonlight made it possible to see. Relief and gratitude filled Dalton. He'd never been so happy to see anyone in his entire life.

"Jake. How can I ever repay you?" He shook his head, smiling from ear to ear. "You've risked your life for me. I'll never forget what you've done."

The two large men filled the small space. Jake's smile mirrored his own feelings. They grinned at each other like fools after downing a jug of whiskey.

"I was glad to oblige, Babcock," Jake replied, then gave a low, subdued laugh that was covered by the wind moving the branches. "I couldn't believe my eyes the first time I saw you in the camp. And wearing prison stripes to boot. I knew something was wrong."

Dalton thoughtfully ran his fingers through the short beard on his face. "Amazing how things work. Me getting shanghaied, and you showing up. The chance meeting is hard to believe. I can't wait to get back to Logan Meadows!"

"Well, we're not there yet. I won't breathe easy until we're *all* on the train." Jake hunkered down, his smile fading. "How do you feel? We can't put you on the train sick; you'd draw attention. We'll have to wait a day or two. Hexum, the man behind all this, has this town buttoned up. They're looking for you. There's no law to go to, and the attendant at the telegraph office can't be trusted. I have a plan, though, one I think will work. I'll lay out my idea, and then you'll be responsible to get yourself to the train on Wednesday morning. Tonight's Sunday. You have enough supplies to last until then and a train ticket. Do you think you can do that?"

Dalton nodded. "You bet I can."

A twig snapped below.

"Adaline?" Dalton mouthed.

Jake shook his head, slowly slipping his gun from the holster. He aimed at the opening and waited.

A boy's head appeared. His eyes went wide, and he was about to bolt when Jake reached out and hauled him inside with a grip on his shirtfront.

"What're you doing, Freddy?" Jake asked, keeping his voice low. "Did anyone follow you?"

Freddy shook his head. "N-no. I snuck out after Mother looked in on me. She thinks I'm asleep. I come out here a lot, and she never knows. Father either." The boy looked Dalton up and down. "This one of the convicts? The one you and Miss Costner broke out?"

Jake looked at Dalton and shrugged. "He eavesdropped on me and Adaline," he said in explanation. "Freddy, have you told anyone about us?"

"No, sir." He shook his head. "I said I wouldn't and I won't."

The kid didn't look as scared now since Jake had holstered his gun. As a matter of fact, he looked the opposite. Like he was having fun.

"Good. I'm glad I can trust you. I have something I need you to do."

Chapter Thirty-One

Jake sat across from his sisters in the Happy Owl Café, a plateful of sausage and eggs on the table before him. Early on Wednesday morning, business was brisk. The warm eatery held savory smells heavy on the air. Outside was sunny and beautiful, and the sight of the foamy green ocean had brought a nice calmness to his soul. Oregon was growing on him, especially this tasty blackberry jam he was eating on his biscuits. It was mighty good.

By some miracle, Monday and Tuesday had passed without incident. Jake saw little of Hexum, and no one came to search the house. The situation was so quiet, Jake's suspicions were on high alert. Out of curiosity, he strolled by the sheriff's office, but the building was vacant. Hexum was in his office, but Strangely wasn't anywhere to be found. The *Tigress* was still moored at the docks.

To Jake's surprise, Wil Lemon hadn't shown his face. Jake wondered if his absence was the reason Courtney was so quiet and glum. He hadn't gone back to the tree house since he'd spoken with Dalton on Sunday night. He'd never seen his friend so thin, but that could be remedied with breakfasts and suppers at the Silky Hen and Nana's Place once they were back in Logan Meadows.

Hoot, hoot, hooooooooooot.

Hearing the train whistle, both of his sisters' gazes cut to Jake's. He winked and they both gave a nod, having worked out a plan. Courtney still didn't know anything about Dalton, but with Wil Lemon to worry about, Jake thought keeping the secret was important. He wouldn't put anything past the man. He might try to cart Courtney off against her will. The less she knew, the better.

Besides, they needed a diversion to get all eyes on them so Dalton, who should by now be waiting on the opposite side of the tracks out of sight, could sneak onto the caboose without drawing any attention. Courtney's family kidnapping her away would have people watching and talking. He hoped she played her role to the hilt.

"Here comes the train," Courtney said, now finished with her breakfast. She smiled at him and patted her lips with her napkin.

Jake withdrew several coins, enough to pay for the three meals, and set them next to his plate. He stood and stretched. "Adaline, what did you want to pick up before we went home?" he said loudly so several people sitting close could hear. "I can't remember."

"A roll of lace from the tailor's. Courtney, will you come help? You're so good at visualizing."

Through the large window, Jake saw the Union Pacific roll to a stop a block away at the train depot, puffs of smoke billowing into the white clouds above.

True to form, Courtney made a face. "I have business at the mercantile. You don't need me, Adaline."

Adaline laid her hand on her sister's arm. "But I do."

"Why don't you go with your sister, Courtney? The errand will only take a minute. After that, you can go to the mercantile."

"I guess."

Watching until his sisters headed to the tailor's shop, the last building on the street directly across from the depot, Jake ambled over to the doorway. The Union Pacific was taking on water. The locomotive engineer barked orders at the train crew. Bags of mail were heaped on the railroad platform. The stationmaster checked his watch.

They had a mere ten minutes at the most. In his pocket, he fingered the tickets, two new ones he'd had the minister buy for him yesterday, fearful that in such a small town, news of the purchases might get back to Lemon or Hexum.

From the doorway of the church on the opposite end of the street, Randall Hensley, the man Jake now trusted completely, nodded back. The reverend jerked his chin in the direction of the saloon.

Jake glanced over.

Several horses were tied in front, the bright orange saddle blankets from the outfit Lemon rode with under each saddle. Would the man make a play to stop them from boarding the train? Was anyone watching? Hexum or his men? Dalton would only have so much time, and Jake had to wait until the very last moment for him and the girls to make their scene. Hearing and seeing would be difficult from the far side of the train.

Jake nodded back, an uneasy sense tickling down his spine.

Hoot, hoot, hooooooooooooot.

Watching the last few passengers board, Jake strode toward the tailor's shop and looked in through the window. Courtney and Adaline were just finishing up. He glanced at the saloon. Then over to the train. Still no Hexum. Perhaps the banker was plotting his own escape before his dirty secret got out.

The conductor standing on the deck glanced at his watch, flicked the lid closed, and stepped onto the train. The time had arrived.

Jake opened the door to the shop. "Come on, girls. We still have some packing to do at the house."

"Don't be so impatient, Jake," Courtney called. "I still have to stop at the mercantile."

Adaline caught his look. In front of the clerk, she took Courtney's elbow and hugged her sister's arm next to her side as she propelled her outside. Turning left, instead of right, with Jake directly behind, a moment passed before Courtney acted surprised. The train was only ten feet away.

Courtney jerked to a stop as steam billowed out from under the wheels and the train began to slowly inch forward. "What are you doing? I don't want to go," she cried loudly. She jerked her arm from Adaline and whirled to retreat.

Instead, Jake scooped her up and slung her over his shoulder. He took three steps and then jogged to keep up with the doorway of the moving train car.

"Come on, Adaline," he called. "You first."

Courtney let out several loud screeches. She beat her fists convincingly on his back. Anyone watching was sure to be startled.

"Put me down this instant, Jake!" she screamed, the sound drowned out by another blow of the train's whistle. "I'll scratch your eyes out if you don't let me go this instant. I'm not going with you. I'm not!"

The depot master pointed. A group of cowboys scowled. Jake chanced a glance to the train platform to see everyone looking their way exactly as they'd planned. Hopefully Dalton was making his move too.

"Easy," he called over his shoulder as he jogged. He would have a difficult time getting them both aboard before the train picked up too much speed. Tightening his grip on his youngest sister, he grasped Adaline with his free hand and pushed her onto the train while he increased his pace. Too late now if Dalton had missed his chance.

Once Adaline was on board and out of his way, he took hold of a hand grip next to the door and lengthened his stride, the speed of the locomotive almost pulling him off his feet. With effort, he struggled to keep his hold on his screaming sister as she pummeled his back. Surging forward, he pulled them both aboard as the train whisked past Newport's last outbuilding and was on its way toward the Willamette Valley.

They'd made it. He prayed Dalton had too. Jake couldn't hold back the happiness he felt. All those years he'd longed to know his pa, and now all he wanted to do was return to the ones he loved.

Standing inside the open door of the train car, Jake widened his stance to keep his balance. He didn't have Wil Lemon to worry about anymore, just the startled conductor who blocked his way.

"What are you doing?" the Union Pacific employee bellowed, his ruddy face darkening. "Kidnapping is against the law."

Jake set Courtney on her feet and jabbed a finger in her face just as she opened her mouth to holler again. "You keep quiet."

"Sir? I ask you again, what's going on?"

Courtney gripped the front of her skirt, jerking the fabric into place with a vengeance. She huffed and sputtered.

Several passengers who'd boarded in Newport watched intently. One woman covered her mouth with a gloved hand, her eyes wide above.

"This is my fifteen-year-old sister," Jake explained. "Our pa passed away, and we're moving. She's reluctant to come along."

"I'm not your sister," Courtney blurted, stamping her foot.

"Half sister then," Jake said, correcting himself.

To his horror, Courtney's eyes filled with tears. She was a darned good actress—or was it more? They wanted to keep everyone's attention so Dalton could make his way to the passenger car and quietly slip inside.

"Can you please stop the train so I can get off?" she begged the conductor. "I don't want to leave my papa's grave."

Oh, she's good. Adaline looked as surprised as he felt.

The woman who'd had her hand over her mouth sprang to her feet. "What have you done to this poor child? Conductor, stop the locomotive. She's been taken against her will."

"Ma'am," Adaline said. "My sister has no one back in town to look after her. My father's dying wishes were we should both go with our brother, Jake."

"I'll handle this," Jake said. He looked at the woman and her husband, who had followed his wife to her feet. Both gripped the back of the seat in front of them to keep their balance.

"I cannot stop the train," the conductor said. "That's impossible."

Jake hated to do this, considering Courtney's sensitive feelings. He looked to the husband. "Have you heard of Wil Lemon?" By the look on his face, he had.

The tall man nodded. "Indeed. What does that ruffian have to do with this young girl?"

"Just about everything," Jake said. "He's filled her head with sugar, and they're plannin' to be married—or so he says. I'm not lettin' Courtney throw away her life."

"I see." The man took his wife's arm. "I'd do the same if I were in your shoes."

The woman blanched. "But, honey . . ."

"It's not our business, Betty. This young man is doing the right thing. Just get comfortable and watch the sights go by."

With the fellow's testimony, the conductor's hostile expression ebbed, replaced with a sympathetic look at Jake. "May I have your tickets, sir?"

Courtney wiped her eyes and swallowed.

Jake regretted bringing Lemon into the conversation, but the conductor had looked as if he were ready to do something drastic. Promising himself he'd apologize to her later, he produced the tickets.

The conductor punched them through. "Thank you," the man said, casting a quick glance at both girls. He moved on.

Courtney headed toward some open seats near the back, and Jake and Adaline followed. She plunked herself down and buried her face in her hands. Jake and Adaline took the seat opposite, facing the back of the car. A sound resembling a sob reached Jake's ears.

"I can't believe this," Courtney said in a small voice. Picking up her face, she looked at her sister. Courtney's cheeks were wet with tears. "How could you, Adaline? I can understand Jake, but not you."

Jake took his handkerchief from his pocket and offered it to her, smiling at two women a few seats away who still watched.

Courtney angrily snatched the cloth from his fingers and wiped her face. "What about all our stuff, and your horse? Are we just leaving everything behind?"

"The reverend's going to help Mrs. Torry ship the things you and Adaline packed, sell the rest, and send us the money, then give anything left over to the needy." Jake made sure he spoke loudly enough for the avid women to hear, and one raised a brow before looking away. "He'll send Joker on as well."

Courtney connected with his gaze. Sorrow and relief resided in her eyes. The hair that had come loose when he'd flung her over his shoulder cascaded down her back.

Was she sorry she'd not listened to her father?

Being a brother isn't easy.

"What will Mrs. Torry think when I don't show up?" She kept at the planned dialogue. "She'll be worried. She won't know what happened and will think the worst."

"She knows," Adaline responded. "Like Jake said, she's helping the preacher with our belongings."

Courtney's face crumpled.

Jake thought her reaction was no longer an act. Leaving the one you'd thought you loved must be difficult, no matter the circumstances. He gave her a lot of credit for coming to her senses and helping. She was a good girl. She just didn't know it, or believe it—yet. He'd make her see. Show her just how special she was. Back in Logan Meadows when he had his feet under him squarely.

After a moment, Courtney turned to the window, effectively shutting out both him and Adaline, lost in her own thoughts.

Jake released a healthy breath and sat back, getting comfortable. He was headed home. Home to Daisy. Arriving with more than he'd left with. How would his sisters adapt to Logan Meadows? More importantly, how long would he have to wait before Wil Lemon showed his hand?

Just as Jake was about to close his eyes, the door at the back of the car opened and Dalton looked in, clean-shaven and dapperly dressed. The last part of the plan had fallen successfully into place.

Chapter Thirty-Two

Daisy could hardly think with all the troubling thoughts weaving in and out of her head. She paced back and forth on the depot decking, unable to stand quietly with the rest of her friends present to welcome Jake home. Wringing her hands, she glanced over her shoulder at the large clock on the dormer of the depot. Would the twelve o'clock train ever pull in?

A man named Jay Merryweather had arrived just yesterday in Logan Meadows with a frightening story. One of Jake, and sisters, and the kidnapping of Dalton Babcock! Of a ship named the *Tigress*, ready to take away men against their will. Mr. Merryweather would have been here sooner, but his train had broken down along the way. He was sick with worry for his new comrades.

A soft touch to her arm brought her around. "Daisy, you'll wear a path in the wood," Tabitha Wade said softly. "Come and sit on the bench. Your pacing won't bring the train any faster."

Tabitha was right, but that didn't change the way Daisy felt.

"It's all so unbelievable," she said. "Jake went to Oregon to find out about his father, not all—"

"And he did find his past. Just think how happy that will make him. I'm sure he'll have a lot to tell once he arrives home.

But if you don't sit, you won't have a bit of energy left to welcome him properly."

Hunter Wade, Tabitha's new husband, still dressed in his usual buckskin shirt and as tall and handsome as ever, joined them. The cool October air—ripe with scents of dried grass wet from last night's rain, ruffled his hair.

The saloon owner smiled at his wife's last statement. "She's right, Daisy. Everything will be fine. These things have a way of working themselves out."

Daisy gazed into the newlyweds' faces, wondering if she'd ever have the chance to marry Jake. He might not be on this train, or tomorrow's, or the next day's. Everyone just thought that and kept filling her with hopeful platitudes. Something could have happened after Mr. Merryweather departed. Jake might have been killed by the guards he'd tricked, and he'd never arrive home again. She wrapped her arms around her middle.

Even though the friends waiting nearby tried to smile as if nothing was wrong, she knew better. Hannah chewed one side of her bottom lip. She only did that when she was undecided about something. Susanna, Brenna, and Jessie pretended to carry on a light discussion, but their hands gripped tightly in front of their skirts said different. They didn't look each other in the eye. The men were straight-faced, speaking quietly with Jay Merryweather, the newcomer and bearer of the bad news.

No, all of Logan Meadows didn't believe what they were feeding her. They were frightened for Jake too.

What would happen if Jake didn't step off the train?

Chapter Thirty-Three

When the train chugged past Three Pines Turn, Jake could hardly contain his excitement. If Jay Merryweather had reached Logan Meadows, someone might be waiting at the depot. And that someone might be Daisy. They hadn't known their exact day of arrival, but one could hope.

He breathed in the crisp mountain air streaming through the open window with its scents of pine, fall, and the coming winter. He marveled at the dark blue cloudless sky, which seemed to go on forever. For the first time ever, the sight reminded him of the Pacific Ocean—deep, mysterious, endless.

Home. A profound pleasure filled him. The tall purple mountains far off in the distance appeared to be saying *hello, welcome back. We've missed you.*

Jake smiled, catching his reflection in the window glass. He'd had an adventure. He'd met his father. Even if he could go back, change things so he'd grown up at his father's side, he wouldn't. This place and these people had been his destiny.

He gazed out on the sweeping pastures past Logan Meadows. This was a wide land, one in which to grow. One where he'd raise his sons and daughters, and pass on the little wisdom he had. They would grow tall and strong. Their roots would be here with him and their mother. Once this train pulled into Logan Meadows, he was never leaving again.

"You better stop smiling like that or your lips might break off."

Jake turned. Dalton, sitting opposite with Adaline next to his side, grinned like a fool. Jake didn't care who knew how he felt.

He reached up and finger-combed his hair. "How do I look? Is my hair too long? Should've gotten a haircut in Newport."

Next to him, Courtney frowned. "When? With all the secret running around you were doing, breaking people out of jail, setting off dynamite, and pretending to be digging for fossils and bones, you didn't have time. A man can only do so much."

Adaline reached across the space and touched her sister's knee. "We told you why we couldn't say anything, Court. We didn't know who we could trust. And if you were questioned, you were safer not knowing anything."

"You couldn't trust me?"

Courtney's gaze challenged, as usual. One thing Jake knew for sure after this trip was he didn't know very much at all. Sisters were complicated. *We couldn't trust Wil Lemon. And for a while, we couldn't trust you either.*

"We did what we had to do, Courtney," he said, feeling very much like an older brother. "Hope someday you'll understand."

"What I understand is you trusted Freddy Bennett more than you did me."

"We didn't have a choice." Adaline shook her head. "He eavesdropped."

Dalton smiled and ran a hand over his clean-shaven face. He actually looked distinguished in James Costner's clothes. "That kid was a godsend. He brought me a razor and mirror, and helped guide me to the train station through the back streets so I wouldn't be seen. Seriously, I owe him a lot."

Courtney shrugged and turned back to the open country passing by. "I'm glad he could help," she said in a distracted tone, unable to hide her sadness.

"I wonder what's been happening in Logan Meadows," Jake said. "We had a newcomer arrive shortly before I left. Claimed half ownership in the Bright Nugget."

Dalton sat forward and barked out a laugh. "No! Kendall must have been fit to be tied. How'd that happen?"

"Kendall owed money to someone, I guess. A big fellow, not someone Kendall could throw around. The way Albert tells it, the two went to blows right there in the sheriff's office. Seeing how things played out will be interesting. Who knows, maybe Hunter Wade, that's his name, got tired of getting the cold shoulder from people and moved on. Remember the new bookstore?"

Dalton nodded, Adaline listened intently, and Courtney just gazed outside.

"Sure I do," Dalton said. "Was owned by the nice spin—ah, um, unmarried woman, Miss Canterbury. She used to wave to me when I went to stand guard at the bank."

"That's right. She's started doing public readings in her shop every Tuesday night. I didn't go because of the letter from our father, and planning my trip to Oregon, but everyone sure seemed to enjoy them, *especially the women*." He looked hopefully at Courtney. "There'll be lots of nice women to meet."

The locomotive slowed and the outskirts of Logan Meadows came into view.

"We're here," Jake announced.

He took in the town he loved. A few houses came into view. He caught a glimpse of the Feed and Seed on the opposite side of the bridge, still off in the distance, and then the festival grounds. The train jerked and brakes screamed. Putting his face close to the glass, he looked forward and spotted a group of townsfolk congregated at the depot, watching the train's approach.

When he noticed the tremor in his hands, he stuffed them in his pocket. He'd never been so excited. He had a name, sisters, and soon he hoped to be holding the woman he loved.

Even before the train stopped, he stood. Courtney looked up into his face. He was home to his loved ones, but she was still mourning her father. She'd lost the man she loved and was moving to a new place. He needed to keep that in mind. Be patient. Loving. Both she and Adaline would have many adjustments in the days and weeks ahead.

The conductor came through, calling out the town. He wasn't the same man Jake had met on the trip west, but he still felt a closeness with him. So much had changed, and so much had stayed the same.

Jake wanted to stride ahead and hop down the steps, but propriety said he should usher his sisters off the train first. He put out his arm, motioning for them to go before him. Since they'd jumped on at the last second, they didn't have any travel satchels to worry about.

A cheer went up when they descended the one step and a crowd of friends rushed forward. But there was only one face he wanted to see.

"Jake!"

He wrapped Daisy in his arms. He loved the little sounds she made as he hugged her tight. *My woman. My love.* She was what life was all about.

He leaned back, taking in the beauty of her porcelain-white skin, soft brown hair, expressive green eyes filled with love. He found her lips, kissing her soundly. She felt so right in his arms. He'd never again let her go. She lifted her hands around his neck and pushed up on her toes, her pent-up passion taking him by storm.

"You're home. Thank you, God, for bringing him back," she gushed. "I love you so much it hurts. I was frightened that—"

His friends pushed in. Their laughter and hands on his back said everything. They jostled and pressed, all trying to get close.

"I love you too, honey," he said against her lips. "Everything worked out. We'll get married and have a wonderful life. I promise."

"Jake," Gabe and Chase said at the same time.

In the next instant, he and Daisy were engulfed in a manly hug, showing him just how much they cared. His throat tightened. He'd quickly looked around but didn't see his mother anywhere. Had she gone home? Left before they'd really gotten to talk?

"Wait a minute here," Dalton called. "I was the one that got shanghaied, and Jake's getting all the attention."

Laughter sounded and everyone crowded around Dalton, welcoming him, asking questions, giving him hugs.

Jake put out an arm and pulled first Courtney and then Adaline to his side. "Everyone," he called out in a proud voice. "These are my sisters, Adaline and Courtney Costner. They were a huge surprise, but I've gotten over it and lived to tell the tale."

More laughter came from the group.

Jake felt his smile fade. "All kidding aside, this trip and meeting the two of them has been a blessing I've yet to wrap my head around. I'm one lucky cowboy."

More cheering, this time welcoming the girls. The two sisters smiled, nodded, and answered the eager questions launched at them. They could handle themselves. Seeing them smiling and at ease brought him pure joy.

He pulled Daisy close to his side, happy the attention was off them. He followed her gaze over to Adaline and Courtney. "You'll like them."

She turned and smiled up into his face. "I know I will."

"Is my moth—"

"Still in Logan Meadows? Yes, she is. There's something you need to know, Jake. A lot has happened while you were away. Your mother was in the mix of it. She was hurt."

Frowning, he straightened.

"She's recuperating at the Red Rooster. Mrs. Hollyhock stayed behind to take care of her. She said for you to come by as soon as you can."

"What happened?"

"The story is long and complicated. I'll fill you in, but not here. Everyone wants to see your smiling face and welcome you home." Daisy went up on tiptoe and kissed his cheek. "And I don't blame them. I'm not amazed at all hearing how you risked your life to save Dalton and Mr. Merryweather." She pulled his arm closer, snuggling into his side. "I love you." She nodded toward Miss Canterbury and Hunter Wade.

Jake followed her gesture at the pair who seemed to be standing awfully close together.

"They got married. Tabitha is now Mrs. Hunter Wade."

When he pulled up in surprised laughter, Tabitha noticed. She came over, followed by her husband.

"Jake," she said. "Welcome home. All the things I'm hearing are amazing."

Jake chuckled, looking back and forth between her and Hunter. "I'm pretty astonished at all I'm hearing about you! Congratulations." He looked at Hunter and extended a hand. "You're a fast worker, Mr. Wade."

"Call me Hunter. And yes, I agree. But then Miss Hoity-Toity wouldn't want me any other way. Besides, she was chasing me too. Was I to let her suffer?"

With pretend offense, Tabitha gave his arm an affectionate rub. "I'll deal with you later, husband of mine. For now, I wanted to say I'm sorry about your mother."

"Daisy was just telling me."

"Let me know if there's anything we can do. Everyone in the town is relieved her injuries weren't worse. But enough of that for now . . ."

"Thank you. I'll do that." Jake shook his head. "There is something I want to ask you. My pa was a lover of the written word." A jab of sadness made him swallow. So much had happened, he hadn't given his father's passing the time he should. "He had bookshelves everywhere. Filled to the brim. I'd guess three or four hundred volumes. They're set to be shipped here within a few weeks. I was wondering if you might want some to sell in your bookstore. We could split the profit. Even a little would sure help my sisters."

Her face lit up like the sun, making him and Hunter laugh.

"I guess that's your answer," Hunter said. "All you have to do is say the word 'books' to get my wife's attention."

"I'd love to, Jake. Some I may buy myself to put into my lending library and others I'd sell. Would that be all right with you?"

"However you want to work the arrangement is fine with us." Jake extended his arm and they shook hands. "I'll get back to you as soon as they arrive."

Chapter Thirty-Four

Having left Adaline and Courtney in the Silky Hen along with Daisy, Dalton, and the rest of their friends to eat, Jake borrowed Gabe's horse and rode out to the Red Rooster to see his mother.

Logan Meadows had been anything but quiet in his absence. Mr. and Mrs. Ling had suffered at the hands of a bounty hunter, their little girl as well. And his ma, she'd been beaten trying to defend them. Storybook Lodge was going through repairs, and Tabitha and Hunter had been married.

Reining up in front of the log-and-chink boardinghouse, he sat on his horse and soaked in the good feeling of home mixed with the grief he felt over his ma's pain. From this week, and the whole of her life. His insides knotted, keeping him in the saddle a few moments longer.

Finally going to the front door, he knocked, hat in hand. He allowed time before knocking again, not wanting to disturb the quiet. Soon the door opened.

"Jake." Mrs. Hollyhock stood before him. Her eyes lit with pleasure and she pulled him into a hug. "It's dang good ta see ya, boy. Welcome home."

"It's good to be here."

Taking his arm, she led him inside where his mother sat by the fire in her bedclothes, a small blanket over her lap. Her bruised face looked painful. Mrs. Hollyhock gave him a small smile and hurried away to her bedroom.

Marlene quickly set down the glass raised to her mouth when he came into the room, and Jake's old suspicions came rushing back. He couldn't keep his eyes from narrowing.

"It's just water, Jake."

Guilt welled inside, and he cut his gaze down to the crackling flame in the hearth. "I'm sorry you were hurt," he said stiffly and shifted his weight from one foot to the other. "How do you feel?"

"I'm mending. Won't be a day or two, and I'll be as good as new."

"That's good."

"So, you met James, your father? Has he passed away?"

Jake nodded.

"I'm sorry for you then. I'm sure you'd like more time with him. Will you tell me anything, or would you rather I didn't ask? I'd like to know, but I'll abide by your wishes."

Still holding his hat, he lowered himself into the chair opposite. He looked into her eyes, something he hadn't done in years. "You deserve to know."

Even in the dim room, he could see her surprise. This was the first time he could remember a conversation with his mother being civil since he'd left her in Valley Springs. She'd always been drunk. Always been angry. Now he understood why.

"Thank you for saying that."

He pictured her as a young woman. Pretty and sweet. Naive of the ways of men. One who fell in love with James Costner all those years ago.

"He was more educated than I expected him to be. Said he was from Michigan, and the family is still there. I have two younger half sisters. I brought 'em back to Logan Meadows. Their ma's been dead for years."

If his ma had questions, she didn't voice them.

"He apologized for leaving you when you told him you were in the family way. Said if he could do things differently, he would."

She dropped her gaze to her hands in her lap.

Hearing this now must be difficult. He wasn't sure. "What I want to know is why you hated *me* so much. When I was a boy. And why you didn't tell me about your past? Before you were a saloon girl? Those facts might have given me some comfort back then. I'm not feelin' sorry for myself; I'd just like to know."

His mother shifted in the chair, and her brows pulled down in pain.

Jake winced. She was hurt more than she was saying.

"At first, I couldn't believe he'd run off. I was scared. I tried writing to him when his boss revealed to me where he'd gone. I prayed he'd change his mind, would come back. But he didn't."

That was a shock. He couldn't believe his ma had ever said a prayer. She always acted so tough and mean.

"After sending a handful of letters, I finally received a reply. He told me to let go. Stop contacting him. Said he had things he needed to do, and they didn't include me." She took a breath.

"Or his child," Jake said what she'd left out.

She nodded. "I didn't want to shame my parents when the baby began to show, so I took what money I had, which was not a small sum, and ran off. When my funds were gone, there was only one thing left for me to do. By then, you were a little tyke."

"That doesn't explain why you were always so angry."

"Every time I looked at you, I saw him. The hurt and betrayal was too much. I drank. Then I drank some more. I'm not saying I wasn't at fault; I just turned into a hate-filled person. I guess I still am."

Jake remembered James's story sounding the same. Didn't change a thing. But now he understood all she had lost because of his father and him, and Jake understood her a little better.

"He told me you came from a good family. Why didn't you go home? Get help? Surely they wouldn't hold one mistake over your head for the rest of your life."

"By the time I realized that's what I should do, I was too far gone. Had lived in a saloon for several years. I wanted to, though. And later, realized doing so would have been much better for you, even with the stigma you would have borne. At least you would have had a proper roof over your head. And hot meals." Her face crumpled for a moment, but she quickly corralled her emotions. "One day just led into another and another until I'd come to this day." She looked around the warm interior of the inn.

"Are your parents still alive?"

"I don't know."

"Maybe that's something you should find out."

For several long moments, she gazed at him.

Moved by a compassion he'd never felt before, Jake reached forward and took one of her hands. It was cold. And rough. Unable to stop himself, he brought her fingers to his lips and kissed them.

Her soft intake of breath moved him even more.

Suddenly he felt lighter, as if a weight he hadn't known he'd been carrying lifted from his shoulders. He hadn't forgiven his father in time, and that was a huge regret. Maybe he would always bear the scars of those childhood wounds, but now they were badges of honor.

"I'm glad you're here," he said, his voice gravelly with emotion. "Maybe we can put the past to bed."

Blinking hard, his mother nodded.

He stood, pulled on his hat, and looked into her misty eyes. "I best be going. Daisy and the girls are waiting."

Chapter Thirty-Five

Three days later, scents of roasting beef lingered on the warm air of the bunkhouse as Jake brought a mug of coffee to the table and sat.

Since his return to work, all the hands wanted to do was talk about his sisters—who, for the time being, were living with Chase and Jessie. Every time Adaline or Courtney came outside, he'd find the ranch hands suspiciously cleaning their gear on the bunkhouse porch, or shaving at the outside mirror.

Sweeping the porch, for gosh sakes. A chore usually belonging to Tater Joe, the cook.

As disconcerting as their behavior was, Jake guessed he understood. The cowhands spent days on end with cattle, rattlesnakes, dirt, and horses. It usually took a trip into town to be able to catch a glimpse of a pretty, young—*single*—girl. This was big news for the Broken Horn.

He took a swig of his coffee and then lowered the mug to the scarred tabletop made from four ten-foot planks. The narrow, but long, piece of furniture took up the center of the room. Courtney's predicament, if she indeed had one, was never far from his thoughts.

Chase came through the door, a large sack of potatoes on his shoulder. The brim of his brown felt hat was pushed up so he'd be able to see in the dimness of the room. His jeans were clean, and the sheepskin jacket he was so fond of covered a pressed shirt. He even had a small red bandanna tied around his neck. His gone-to-town attire.

"Aww, Jake, just the man I wanted to see." He glanced around at the nearly empty room, seeing only Tater Joe there with Jake. "Where is everyone?"

Jake chuckled. "Out earning their pay, boss. Tyler and Gabe just lit out for the pasture. I'm headed that way soon myself."

"In a minute." Chase went to the stove, deposited the sack on the floor, and filled a cup with coffee. Straddling the bench, he faced Jake. "How's the groom-to-be? Your wedding day will be here before you know it."

"Good. And yes. I know."

"Getting nervous?"

"Nope. Not a bit. Just excited."

Chase took a loud slurp. "Good man. Thought as much." Pride shone in his eyes. "Between your sisters and my wife, we haven't had a private moment to talk. How'd the situation go in Newport? I'd like to know."

Jake had known this moment would come. "First, let me thank you again for taking in Adaline and Courtney. Until we find—"

"They can stay forever as far as Jessie and I are concerned. We told you that, Jake. Quit your worryin'. Jessie and Sarah are thrilled to have more fillies in the house. Those two haven't quit their chatter since they arrived. Having new things to discuss is always nice, and Adaline does have some funny stories. Shane sure has taken to 'em." Chase took another sip, quieter this time.

"Don't worry about Courtney. She'll come around. She's just homesick. Can't be easy leaving the only home you've known."

That's not the half of it. "She's awful glum. I told you Lemon might be following. I don't like putting Jessie in danger, or anyone else."

"We've faced dangers together before, Jake. I wouldn't expect anything different now. We'll manage. Then again, this fella might be all bark and no bite, and you and Courtney have seen the last of him. That'd be more like it." He took off his hat and scratched the back of his head. "I saw Gregory Hutton when I dropped the moppets off at school today. He's looking forward to having Courtney in class—when she's ready, of course."

That's good. Another hurdle cleared.

"Now, tell me about your pa. Was there time for you to get to know him?"

Jake gazed down at the last of his coffee in the bottom of his cup.

"Jake?"

"Not much."

Chase nodded.

"He was born and raised in Sunnyside, Michigan. His family runs a mercantile. James wanted to be a writer. Liked books. Took a job in some other town, hoping to do just that. Met my ma. She turned up expectin', and he skedaddled. Ended up with some kind of cancer the doctors couldn't fix."

Chase grunted. They sat in silence for several minutes, listening to Tater Joe peel the supper potatoes.

So much about his father he still didn't know. "He had dreams. Got scared. Said, in the end, he didn't achieve nothin'. It's sad in a way. I wish he had."

"That's big of you."

"Not really. Just a fact that feels righter than wrong."

"More coffee, boss? Jake?" Tater Joe called over. "I'm getting ready to toss this black sludge out the door, unless either of you want it."

"No, thanks," they both responded.

Chase reached out and took Jake's shoulder. The contact felt good. Firm.

"What's eating you?" he asked.

Jake swallowed, suddenly feeling like he was suffocating in his own body. Then he felt five years old, and a moment later, on the edge of dying himself.

"James wanted forgiveness and I didn't give it. I couldn't, Chase. Not at the time. One minute later, he was gone. Just like that. He was gone."

Chase's grip tightened. "Don't beat yourself up. As God is my witness, I swear your pa understood why you held back. Your presence there was all he needed to know how you felt. Trust me on this."

A pitiful sound forced its way out of Jake's throat, embarrassing him. Emotion shook his body, and he cut his gaze away from Chase, but it was too late, he'd seen. He knew.

"Ain't no crime to feel, Jake. None at all. You did good. And you're doing more good by taking in Adaline and Courtney." Chase stood. "You best get back to work now. Strenuous exertion is good for the soul. Then take off early and go into town. Step out with Daisy. She may be getting nervous herself and needs some calming."

Jake nodded and dashed at the moisture in his eyes, thankful Chase was his friend. What a blessing to come back to this ranch, to people who loved him. Jake wouldn't trade that for anything.

Chapter Thirty-Six

Dalton relaxed in the middle of the third pew on the groom's side of the church, thankful to be back in Logan Meadows. The alternative was just too unthinkable, and he had a hard time believing the last few weeks of his life. Jay Merryweather sat on his right, wearing his crooked single-lens glasses that he'd reshaped as best he could.

Rumor was only a few close friends and family had been invited to attend the service, but as time grew close for the ceremony to start, the church had begun to fill. Within a few minutes, all the pews were completely occupied. A handful of cowboys, Jake's comrades from the ranch, stood in the back of the nave by the double doors, their clothes protected from the blustery weather and intermittent rain on this fifteenth day of November by long leather coats.

Rumor also spread that the wedding had been postponed over two weeks so Jake's mother could heal enough to attend. She sat in the front row, beside Jake's sisters and Mrs. Hollyhock. Next to her was Jessie Logan with a fidgety Shane on her lap.

Jake stood at the front of the church along with his best man, Gabe Garrison, and Reverend Wilbrand. He wore a black suit, white shirt, and string tie. He'd never looked so polished and sincere, his hands folded in front of his wide stance.

Emotion swirled. That young man had pretty darn near saved his life. Dalton owed him a lot, and not just the money he'd repay for all the expense involved in breaking him out. He blinked several times when something stung in his eyes. He brushed the feeling away, thinking he was becoming a sentimental old fool.

Hunter Wade, sitting on his other side, looked over. "Something wrong, Babcock?" he quietly asked, a half smile pulling his lips.

Dalton didn't know the man well enough to tell him to mind his own business. He shook his head, and then his eyes widened when Adaline stood and sneaked back to his third-row seat. She waited at the end of the pew, looking very pretty—*and young*—in a blue-and-white dress. Seemed she wanted to squish in between him and Hunter.

Mr. Harrell, on the very end of the pew, stood and stepped out so she could climb in past Mrs. Harrell, Maude, Beth, Julia, Nell, Maddie, Charlie, Tabitha, and Hunter.

She wiggled in and got comfortable, then smiled up into his face. "I hope you don't mind."

"Not at all," Dalton whispered back. "I thought you might be part of the wedding party."

"Daisy asked both Courtney and me, but we felt it best she and Jake stick to their original plan. Courtney and I know so few people, this feels much better anyway." She took a deep breath, then let it out, her eyes bright with excitement. "Have you heard the news?"

"What?"

"The sheriff came out to the ranch this morning. What's his name, Albert Preston?"

Dalton nodded.

"He's heard back from the US marshal he notified by telegram. Seems Hexum got so rattled when he couldn't find you or Mr. Merryweather, he actually sailed away on the *Tigress*. Told his employees he had to go check on his business holdings in Alaska." She gave a small, quiet laugh. "He won't be safe there. The law is on his tail. And they'll free all the others who have been forced to work in his mine."

"I suppose Strangely and the others sailed away too."

"I don't know," she whispered back. "He didn't say anything about them. I'm surprised he didn't tell you himself."

"I've been busy."

"Oh?"

"Yeah. Figuring on what I'm going to do with the rest of my life. I've sent some telegrams. My kind landlady is sending my few belongings to Logan Meadows, and my bank is wiring my funds into Mr. Lloyd's bank. Jay, here, has been offered a job in the haberdashery by Mr. Harrell. He's staying on too."

Another smile blossomed on Adaline's face. She reached across him and touched Jay's arm. "I'm happy to hear that, Mr. Merryweather."

The man smiled and nodded.

Dalton couldn't miss the mistiness of Adaline's eyes when she sat back. He tilted his head in question.

"Weddings always touch my heart," she explained. "This one more than ever. It's my brother's. The brother I never knew I had until a few months ago. Look at him, Dalton. He's incredibly handsome, but more, he's kind and thoughtful ..." She swallowed hard. "He watches out for Courtney and me. My heart trembles when I think about how much I love him."

At Adaline's heartfelt declaration of love, Dalton couldn't stop himself from staring into her face. She was young and beautiful. *Young* being the word he should remind himself of whenever he found himself feeling this way. He covered her hand with his and gave a gentle squeeze before returning his own to his lap.

"And I'm sure he feels the same way about you."

Jake gazed around the sanctuary, totally at ease since the day had finally arrived. All these people, his *friends*, were here for him and Daisy. The fact seemed quite remarkable.

Their quiet, intimate family wedding had turned into something somewhat different. Every seat was filled and his chums from the ranch stood at the back, looking very respectable in their Sunday go-to-meeting shirts, pants, and string ties. More than one head of hair was combed nicely and there was not a hat to be seen.

His good pal, Tyler Weston, caught his eye, nodding. Jake couldn't hold back a smile. Dalton might have some competition there for Adaline, not that his sister or friend even knew their feelings yet. The thought brought a surge of sadness for Courtney. Would she ever get the chance to be wooed and courted? She was so young.

He glanced her way in the front pew to find her looking right at him, almost as if she'd been waiting to catch his attention. A smile like he'd not seen before appeared on her face. She slowly moved her head back and forth, her cheeks turning pink before she averted her gaze.

Courtney! The happiness that had been shadowed by the possibility of her predicament burst out. This would be a day to remember for more reasons than one.

The place quieted when Eddie Brinkley, Mrs. Brinkley's oldest grandson stationed in a front corner of the church, put his fiddle under his chin and drew the bow slowly across the strings. A sweet sound filled the room.

Jake watched with a full heart as Philomena came down the aisle, carrying a candle wrapped in a white ribbon and tied with a bow. Daisy had insisted her friend be in the wedding and would not be swayed no matter how much Philomena had argued it wouldn't be proper.

The saloon girl walked slowly to the pleasing sound of the violin, a small smile on her lips. She didn't make eye contact with anyone as she came. Once she was in front, she took her place on the bride's side of the altar.

Next came Sarah, all little-girl smiles. Her gaze darted around the watching faces, looking for her ma. Jessie stood for a moment so her daughter could find her. When she did, Sarah's smile grew. Her little hands carried a small bundle of some sort of greenery they'd found somewhere, also tied up with a bow.

When she was almost to the front, she looked at Jake with the sweetest expression, transporting him back to when he was a kid, just meeting her and Gabe for the first time in Mrs. Hollyhock's mercantile in Valley Springs—right after Chase and Jessie had married. She'd been a cute little moppet. And now look at her, a little girl going on young lady. Those days felt like a moment ago, and yet five years had passed . . .

He glanced up and his breath caught. Daisy was a vision, gliding down the aisle on Chase's arm. His shy young bride looked stunning in a wispy lavender dress adorned with ribbons and lace. Her eyes shone with adoration. If Chase hadn't had a hold of her, she looked as if she might have floated away with happiness.

Jake was glad he made her happy. Her life hadn't been easy from the get-go—and her past was a time he didn't like to contemplate. If he could move heaven and earth to give her a good life, he'd do it. And thank God every day for the privilege.

In a fog of pleasure, Jake smiled as Chase handed Daisy over, and she placed her small, delicate hand in the bend of his arm. Chase bent down and softly kissed her cheek with fatherly pride.

"Who gives this woman to be married," Reverend Wilbrand asked.

"I do," Chase replied in a clear, strong voice, then went to sit beside Jessie.

Reverend Wilbrand smiled kindly at Daisy and Jake. "Please join hands."

They did.

"We're gathered here in the sight of God and man to join these two young people in marriage. Holy matrimony is a sacrament given by God, to be cherished and nurtured through good times and in bad, through sickness and in health. Never to be taken for granted or put aside. Do you, Jake Costner, take Daisy Smith to be your lawfully wedded wife, to have and to hold, remaining faithful to her from this day forward, for so long as you both shall live?"

Jake smiled into Daisy's face. So much had happened. He'd come so far to arrive at this beautiful young woman before him. "I do," he said in a strong voice, leaving no room for her to doubt.

"Do you, Daisy Smith, take Jake Costner to be your lawfully wedded husband, to have and to hold, remaining faithful to him from this day forward, for as long as you both shall live?"

Her eyes twinkled and she smiled. "I do."

Jake liked her soft, sentimental tone. He rubbed a thumb over her fingers, and her eyes softened even more.

"The ring, please."

Gabe handed the ring to Reverend Wilbrand, who in turn, blessed the delicate band and placed it in Jake's palm. The immensity of the church wedding, their pledges of love, his unbending commitment, it all meant so much, especially in light of his parents' history. The ceremony was a beautiful thing—*they* were a beautiful thing.

Jake slipped the ring onto Daisy's trembling finger with all the care in the world.

"Jake and Daisy," Reverend Wilbrand said. "Always remember the hands you hold today are the same ones you'll hold throughout your life. They'll comfort you in sorrow and lift you up in happiness. Never forget the love you feel today."

They gazed at each other until a crack of thunder overhead broke the spell.

"Very good. By the powers vested in me by the Territory of Wyoming, I now pronounce you husband and wife. You may kiss the bride."

Daisy lifted her face and Jake softly, reverently, kissed her lips.

The room went silent in awe.

"Kiss 'er harder, Jake," Shane called out.

Jessie looked horrified. Smiles broke out, people were nodding and talking. Shane looked plenty proud of himself as Chase lifted him from his mother's lap onto his own.

Jake, only too happy to oblige, wrapped Daisy in his arms.

"I love you, Daisy," he whispered against her lips. "I'll do everything in my power to make you happy."

Then, as if in a dream one fears would never come, and feeling like a different man from the one who'd headed for Oregon and his history, Jake dipped Daisy low and covered her lips with his.

~~~Author's Note~~~

Dear Readers, thank you for reading Where Wind Meets Wave. As the author, I enjoyed the change of scenery. I had fun writing the coastal town and seeing the differences of the two settings from Jake's prospective. For the sake of the story, I had to move the Yaquina Bay train depot three miles farther west from its original location and place it in Newport. My restaurants, businesses, streets, and citizens are fictional. Other than that, the details of Newport and the Yaquina Bay lighthouse are historically accurate.

Acknowledgements

I so enjoyed bringing Jake's story to life in Where Wind Meets Wave. In the process, I have many people to thank for their help. My brilliant, trusted editors, Pam Berehulke and Linda Carroll-Bradd, who have taught me much over the years. My first reader, Saralee Etter, who spots plot holes and missed opportunities before the book is shipped off for editing. My excellent team of beta readers—you know who you are. Kelli Ann Morgan for the beautiful cover. Bob Houston for the formatting. My family, for their support, encouragement, and plotting abilities. My writer friends who are living this wonderful awesome adventure with me. The delightful Eleanor Siebers, Bureau of Land Management ranger at the Yaquina Head Lighthouse, for her insight and knowledge of the rich history of the area and timelines. Tami, at the Lincoln County Historical Society, for a rainy day of fun and information. Always to my readers for enriching my life. To our God for His rich blessings.

Thank you!

About The Author

Caroline Fyffe was born in Waco, Texas, the first of many towns she would call home during her father's career with the US Air Force. A horse aficionado from an early age, she earned a Bachelor of Arts in communications from California State University-Chico before launching what would become a twenty-year career as an equine photographer. She began writing fiction to pass the time during long days in the show arena, channeling her love of horses and the Old West into a series of Western historicals. Her debut novel, *Where the Wind Blows*, won the Romance Writers of America's prestigious Golden Heart Award as well as the Wisconsin RWA's Write Touch Readers' Award. She and her husband have two grown sons and live in the Pacific Northwest.

Want news on releases, giveaways, and bonus reads? Sign up for Caroline's newsletter at: www.carolinefyffe.com
See her Equine Photography: www.carolinefyffephoto.com
LIKE her FaceBook Author Page: Facebook.com/CarolineFyffe
Twitter: @carolinefyffe
Write to her at: caroline@carolinefyffe.com

Made in the USA
Middletown, DE
07 February 2017